Good Night Gunslinger . . .

The light from the hall did little to illuminate the room, and he was at more of a disadvantage because the man inside already had his night vision. Clint drew his gun and went in low. The first muzzle flash showed him where the man was, and the second flash was the man's gun discharging into the ceiling as Clint's shot hit him.

The shot flung the man backward and as he hit the window the glass gave and he flew out into midair. He and the glass crashed to the street together. Clint took a moment to light the lamp in the room and then walked to the street. Several people had gathered around the fallen man.

"Somebody call the sheriff, please?"

A man looked up and said, "What for?"

Also in THE GUNSMITH series

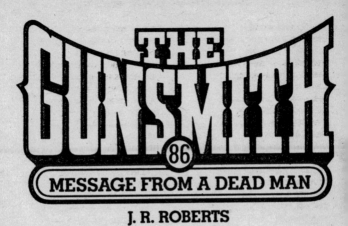

THE GUNSMITH

86

MESSAGE FROM A DEAD MAN

J. R. ROBERTS

JOVE BOOKS, NEW YORK

THE GUNSMITH #86: MESSAGE FROM A DEAD MAN

A Jove book / published by arrangement with
the author

PRINTING HISTORY
Jove edition / February 1989

ISBN: 0-515-09926-0

Jove books are published by The Berkley Publishing Group,
200 Madison Avenue, New York, New York 10016.
The name "JOVE" and the "J" logo
are trademarks belonging to Jove Publications, Inc.

PRINTED IN THE UNITED STATES OF AMERICA

10 9 8 7 6 5 4 3 2 1

ONE

Clint Adams was on the road to Weston, Arizona, but his mind was still back in the town he'd just left, Doby. It wasn't so much the town he was thinking about as it was a certain young lady with whom he'd formed a rather close physical relationship during his stay there . . .

He'd met Nancy Calvin when he'd gone to the hardware store for a spade. He'd broken the one he carried in his wagon when he'd lodged a wheel in a mud puddle. He had used the spade to free the wagon, but the wooden handle had snapped, and the spade itself had gotten bent out of shape.

Nancy had been behind the counter when he entered, and there had been a mutual, immediate attraction. (She had told him this later, and he believed her because he thought he had noticed something right off.)

She had been a medium-tall girl, about five-five or so, with brown hair cut real short, like a boy. In fact, she had been standing with her back to him and he had thought just that, that she was a slender boy—but then, the counter had kept him from seeing her shapely bottom, which had been encased in tight jeans. When she turned around, however, there was no longer any question. She had big, liquid brown eyes, a small nose, and a bee-stung mouth with full, pouty lips. Her waist was so slim that it made the proud, thrusting little breasts seem larger than they actually were. In reality, they were no larger than a couple of juicy peaches.

She had waited on him, helping him find just the right spade, which proved an arduous task, indeed. So difficult had it been, in fact, that he told her he thought she deserved a dinner for all the time she had spent with him. She agreed and made a date to meet at six that evening.

By eight, they were in her bed . . .

Clint was just getting to the part where he had removed her shirt to expose those luscious, peach-sized breasts when Duke started kicking up a storm, intruding on his thoughts.

''Whoa,'' he said, reining the team to a stop. ''What's going on, Duke?'' he shouted, dropping down to the ground.

He walked around behind the rig, where Duke was tied off.

''What is it, fella?'' he asked, stroking the big gelding's massive neck.

Duke exhaled forcefully, his nostrils rippling, and then tossed his head. Clint stepped back to avoid being accidently knocked down.

Something was obviously upsetting Duke, and Clint

became wary. The horse's instincts were rarely wrong, and Clint trusted them as much as he trusted his own.

"All right, boy, all right," he said, trying to calm the horse down. "I'll have a look around. Stand easy, shh," he said, rubbing Duke's nose.

As Clint stepped back Duke lifted his head and his nostrils rippled again. There was something in the air that the animal didn't like the smell of.

Just in case there was trouble brewing, Clint untied the reins that held Duke to the rig. If lead started flying, he didn't want Duke to be trapped.

He loosened his gun in its holster and then began to look around. He found what was bothering Duke about twenty feet off the road to what would have been his right as he sat behind the team.

"I see," he said, falling to one knee.

At first he thought the man was dead. There was too much blood across the front of his shirt for him not to be, but amazingly he was not. Clint detected a slight rising and falling of his chest, and when he put his ear to the man's chest he could just make out the beat of his heart.

He appeared to have been shot in the stomach, a wound that there was very little chance of surviving. The best thing he could do for the man would be to put a bullet in his head, like a horse with a broken leg, but things just didn't work that way.

"Somebody went to a lot of trouble to kill you, friend," Clint said, "and now it looks like I'm going to go to a lot to try and keep you alive."

He ran to the rig to find something he could use to clean and bind the man's wounds. He also took one

of his water canteens. He'd move the rig off the road
as soon as he was able to do something to staunch the
man's bleeding.

He pulled the man's shirt open to expose the wound,
which was as ugly as any he had ever seen.

"Before we can even clean it," he said to the man,
who couldn't hear him, "we've got to try and control
that bleeding as much as we can."

He packed the wound with cloth and then tied it
down, wrapping it all the way around the man. He
pulled it as tight as he could get it and hoped it would
work. Next, he bathed the man's face with water.
From the feel of him he was burning up from fever,
and from the look of him he had been beaten up pretty
good before—or after—he'd been shot, most likely
before.

"All right, friend," he said, standing up, "let me
get my rig over here and we'll see what we can do
about making you more comfortable."

Most likely, he thought as he walked to the rig,
I'm just fixing it so that this fella can die more comfortably.

TWO

Nancy Calvin's skin was as smooth as a calfskin glove, and she smelled like lilacs in the spring.

Immediately after removing her shirt he noticed that her nipples were already hard—as hard as peach pits. He'd nibbled them for a time, and as he did she had unbuttoned her own pants and slid them off. After that she worked on his clothing, and they finally had to step back and give each other room to finish undressing. After that, however, there was no holding back. They had tumbled to her bed together, mouths fused together, her tongue blossoming sweetly into his mouth, her nails raking his back.

"Oh, damn," she had breathed into his ear, "oh, yes, put it in now, please . . . oh, please . . ."

He slid atop her in reply to her pleading and when he slid into her she was as hot and liquid as a—

"Ohhh . . ."

Phil Sadler's moan jerked Clint back to the present.

"How you doing, Phil, ol' boy?" he asked, leaning over the man, but there was no answer.

After moving his rig and freeing the horses of their

5

burden so they could rest, Clint had gone through the
man's pockets to try and identify him. He found a
letter in the man's shirt pocket, and although it was
covered with blood he was able to make out that it
was addressed to "Phil Sadler." From that point on
he started calling the man Phil. The man was in no
condition to object.

Going through the rest of his pockets he found nothing. The absence of anything from his pockets—espe-
cially money—led Clint to believe that the man had
been robbed. There were signs about that more than
one horse had been present, so he could only assume
that Sadler had been waylaid by several riders, who
had shot him, robbed him, and stole his horse, leaving
him for dead.

Clint used water from his canteen to bathe the man's
face, but the fever would not go down.

It was dark now and he had a fire going. Sadler
had already lasted longer than he had expected, and
Clint wondered what would happen if the man made
it through the night.

He had thought it inadvisable to move the man.
Doby and Weston were roughly equidistant from
where they had stopped, a bumpy ride on the rig would
have killed the man for sure before they reached either
town.

"I'll tell you something, Phil, boy," Clint said,
pulling the man's blanket up higher, "if you make it
through this night, you might just be strong enough
to make that trip in the morning. I wish you luck."

Luck, however, was not with Phil Sadler.

•   •   •

It was about 4 A.M. when Clint became aware of Sadler. The man's hand was opening and closing on the ground, as if he were trying to grab on to something.

"Sadler," he said, reaching for the man's hand. Convulsively, Sadler's hand closed on his, holding it tight, as tight as a death grip, Clint couldn't help thinking.

The man's throat worked, and using his other hand, Clint brought the canteen over. He worked the top off and gave the man some water.

"Don't try to talk," Clint said, but the man seemed intent on making the effort.

"Is your name Phil Sadler?"

The man's face became contorted with pain for a moment and then he nodded.

"Who shot you, Sadler?" Clint asked. "Who did it?"

"No—" Sadler said, then tried again, "No time— find Leggett—"

"What?" Clint said, leaning closer to the man's mouth. "What did you say?"

"Leggett," Sadler said, "f-find Harrison Leggett—"

"Harrison Leggett," Clint said. "I've got the name. Where, Sadler, where do I find him?"

"P-Pinnacle—" Sadler said, his voice a harsh whisper now. Clint could hear death in the man's voice. "P-Pinnacle!"

"Arizona?" Clint asked. "Is Pinnacle in Arizona?"

The man nodded.

"And what do I tell this Leggett fella?"

"Tell him—don't tell anyone else—tell him—" Sadler stammered. His lips moved then, and Clint couldn't hear him.

"What? What?" Clint asked, leaning over until his ear was almost touching the man's lips. "Say it again, Sadler."

Sadler repeated it, and Clint was just barely able to make out the words before the death rattle crept into his ear, and he sat up abruptly to get away from it.

He buried Phil Sadler on the spot and marked the grave as well as he could with some stones and a cross fashioned from tree limbs.

The man's last words meant nothing to Clint Adams, but he hoped they would mean something to Harrison Leggett of Pinnacle, Arizona.

It would be a shame for Phil Sadler to have died for nothing.

THREE

When Clint arrived in Weston two days later he left his rig and Duke in the care of the liveryman and obtained directions to the sheriff's office.

"Got some trouble?" the man asked.

"Not that I know of," Clint said, and left to follow the directions.

He found the sheriff's office and entered without knocking. The man behind the desk was white-haired and big-bellied and wore a sheriff's star on his chest. He was eating his lunch and looked up at Clint in annoyance.

"Yeah?" The single word was a demand, and Clint immediately disliked the man.

Maliciously, Clint took out the bloody letter he'd taken from Phil Sadler's pocket and tossed it on the desk.

"Hey!" the lawman cried, rearing back from the stained piece of paper. "What the hell—"

"Took that out of a dead man's pocket, Sheriff, just before I buried him. Maybe it'll help you contact his next of kin."

9

Clint doubted that. The only thing readable on it had been Phil Sadler's name. Even the address where he'd received it had been obliterated, as well as a return address. The letter inside had yielded little else.

"Hey, wait a dang minute!" the sheriff said as Clint started for the door.

Clint stopped and turned around.

"You can't just come waltzing in here and drop somethin' like that on me."

"Not while you're eating lunch, right?"

"Huh? Yeah, right. What's your name, fella?"

"Adams," Clint said. "Clint Adams."

It was one of the few times that Clint hoped someone would recognize his name—and his hope was granted. As the name sank in the old lawman's eyes widened and he stared at Clint openly.

"Uh, the, uh, the Gunsmith?"

"So they say."

"I see," the man said. He stood up and said, "I hope, I, uh, didn't insult you, uh, Mr. Adams—"

Clint refrained from telling the man that he insulted the badge he was wearing.

"No offense taken, Sheriff."

"Oh, well, thanks," the man said, pausing to moisten his dry lips. "Could I, uh, ask you where you found this fella?"

"On the road between here and Doby," Clint said. "He was gutshot and left to die. I sat up with him half the night."

"Took him a long time to die, eh?"

"Longer than anybody deserves," Clint said. He always thought that dying ought to be quick, before a man had time to think about it.

"Yeah, I guess . . ." the sheriff said.

"What's your name, Sheriff?"

"Huh, me? Masters, Owen Masters."

"Been sheriff here long?"

"Nigh onto eight years, now."

That was a long time for one sheriff to serve. Clint couldn't believe that a better man hadn't come along during that time. Maybe it was simply that no one else wanted the job.

"You ever hear of this fella?"

Masters peered down nervously at the blood-stained envelope on his desk, trying to read the name.

"Sadler," Clint said, "Phil Sadler."

"Sadler, Sadler," the sheriff said, rubbing his jaw, which was covered with a snowy white beard, "no, can't say as I have."

"How about Leggett," Clint said, "Harrison Leggett. Ever heard of him?"

"Leggett?" the sheriff said, rubbing his jaw again. "Nope, that don't ring a bell, neither."

Apparently neither Sadler nor Leggett was a well-known figure in Arizona.

"Well, Sheriff Masters, I really don't think you're going to get any kind of an address from that letter. Just make a note that I buried Phil Sadler halfway between here and Doby this morning. Maybe somebody will ask you about it in the future."

"Sure thing, Mr. Adams," Masters said. "I'll do that."

As Clint started for the door the sheriff said, "You mind if I ask how long you'll be staying in Weston?"

"Just until morning," Clint said. "I want to give my horses some rest, get a good meal and some sleep in a real bed, and then continue on."

"Well, I hope you enjoy your stay."

"Yeah."

Clint finally got to the door and then turned to face the sheriff again.

"You know a town called Pinnacle?"

"Sure," Masters said, "about five or six days' ride from here. Couple of towns between here and there. Depending on how long you stop in 'em, might take you longer."

"Thanks."

"If you're looking for a good meal, try Rose's Cafe, up the street," the man called after him. "That's where I got this here lunch."

"Thanks again," Clint said, and left.

He went to the hotel first to get a room, then took the sheriff up on his suggestion to try Rose's Cafe.

The size of the man's belly indicated that he knew where the good food was in town.

FOUR

The sheriff had been right about the food in the cafe, it had been excellent.

Rose was a large, middle-aged woman with black hair she kept in a bun behind her head. She was smart enough to have her daughters as the waitresses while she stayed in the kitchen and cooked. It just so happened, however, that Rose was out front when Clint entered, and she took an instant liking to him.

"Just passing through?" she asked him, showing him to a table in the full cafe. It was after normal lunch hours, but the place was still full. Rose always kept a table empty, however, just in case a good-looking stranger came in. She was forever looking for a husband for her daughters.

"That's right."

"Well, I'm Rose and you've come to the right place for a good meal."

"That's what the sheriff told me."

"That water buffalo," she said, laughing. "He's not much of a lawman, but he knows where to go for the best food in town, I'll give him that."

13

"Well, what would you suggest?" he asked.

"The specialty of the house," she said, "and to make it even more special I'll have my daughter serve it."

"Fine," Clint said. He watched as Rose walked back to the kitchen, a huge woman whose flesh bulged, and wondered what her daughter would look like.

In the kitchen both of her daughters were busy filling orders.

"Eligible stranger outside, girls," Rose said.

"Is he good-looking?" Rachel asked. At nineteen she was the youngest and, unlike her mother, was slender and pretty.

"He sure is."

"That means he's for Rachel, right?" Reena asked. Reena was a few years older than Rachel—almost twenty-three now—and favored her mother. She was a big girl, not as fat as her mother, but certainly heavy enough to be called fat. However, both girls had long black hair and smooth skin that was equally beautiful.

"You never know when you'll find a man who likes big girls," Rose told her. "Why don't you both go out there and wait on him."

"All right," Rachel said, "but I'll bet he'll like me better than Reena."

Rose patted her older daughter on the back and said, "Don't listen to her."

"She's right, Momma," Reena said. "Men just don't like fat women."

"That's nonsense," Rose said. "Look at your

father and me. Rest his soul, he never looked at another woman."

"But Momma," Reena said, "Poppa was fat, too."

Rose frowned and said, "Go out there and wait on that man, Reena."

"Yes, Momma."

Clint was flattered by the attention he received from both girls. He had to admit that the younger woman, Rachel, certainly had the better figure. Reena was not as large as her mother, but she was sure a big girl. Still, she did have some redeeming qualities that a less observant man than Clint Adams might not have noticed.

Clint liked women in all sizes and shapes, and never judged them by what was on the surface. Rachel might have had the nicer body, but Reena seemed to have a nicer personality, as well as the prettier eyes. In fact, if Reena's face had been slimmer, she might have been the prettier of the two.

The food was so good that Clint even went back there for dinner. Again, it was later than the usual dinner hour, and this time it wasn't as busy as before. As a result, while Rachel was posing and preening for Clint, Reena was talking to him and making sure he had what he wanted.

As a result, Clint left wondering what Rachel would be like in bed, but genuinely liking Reena better.

After dinner he went to the saloon for a beer, and decided to ask the bartender if he recognized either of the two names he'd asked the sheriff about.

The bartender, a tall, cadaverous-looking man with dark circles under his eyes, rubbed his dark-stubbled jaw and said, "Nope, can't say as I know either one of them fellers. Are they in trouble?"

"One of them isn't," Clint said. "He's dead."

"Oh yeah?" the man said. "Which one?"

"What does that matter to you?" Clint said. "You don't know them."

Clint took his beer in hand and turned around to survey the place. It was one of the two saloons in town, and it was a decent-sized one. It was dark out, and as with most towns, many of the men in town had taken up refuge here from work, or wives, or girlfriends, and would probably stay until the place closed.

There were still some tables left, and Clint chose the one farthest from the front door and sat facing the room so he could see everything.

There wasn't much to see. There were no girls working the place, and he had no way of knowing if this was normal or not. There were a couple of poker games going on, but neither piqued his interest. The players were mostly townspeople who were whiling away the time, and he didn't feel inclined to take their money. There would be no sport in it.

He had a second beer and finally tired of watching the time go by. He decided to turn in and get an early start in the morning.

He left his empty mug on the bar and bid the bartender good-night.

"Another beer?" the bartender asked. "On the house?"

Clint paused and looked at the man who, despite the fact that it wasn't particularly warm in the place, was sweating.

"No, thanks," Clint said. "I've had enough."

"How about—" the man started to say, but Clint waved him off and left.

He'd remember later that the man was sweating.

As Clint left the saloon someone stepped out of the shadows toward him. He turned and saw Rose's youngest daughter, Rachel, sauntering over to him.

"Well, good evening," he said.

"You know," she said to him, "I could tell right from the beginning that you were a gentleman."

"Oh. How did you know that?"

"You never asked me to come to your room with you."

"Well, we just met," he said.

"Yes, but you're a stranger and you'll be leaving town soon."

"Tomorrow, as a matter of fact."

"You see?" she said. "If we both waited, we'd never find out what it would be like."

"So you decided to make the first move."

She smiled dazzlingly and said, "I wouldn't want you to miss anything, Mr. Adams."

It wasn't a very modest thing for her to say. It implied that it was Clint who was missing out, and not Rachel.

"Where's your sister?"

"My fat sister, you mean," Rachel said. "She's probably in bed all alone, crying her eyes out. Come on, honey," she said, linking her arm into his, "we're wasting time."

"Rachel," Clint said, disengaging her arm from his, "I don't think this is a very good idea."

"Why not?"

"Well, to tell you the truth, I'd rather spend time with your sister than you. She's a much nicer person."

Rachel stared at him, genuinely dumbfounded.

"You're kidding."

"No, I'm not."

"But . . . but look," she said, running her hands down over her body. Any other man would have grabbed her and dragged her to his room, and maybe Clint was foolish not to, but he just didn't want to spend time with her. After they made love she'd probably start talking about herself.

"I'm sorry, Rachel," he said, "but I'm just not interested."

He turned and started walking toward the hotel, leaving a totally stunned Rachel standing in front of the saloon.

Just for the sake of her own ego, she might have ended up grabbing the first man who came out—and he would be welcome to her.

Clint collected his key from the desk clerk and went up to the second floor. When he got to his door he started to put the key in the lock when he stopped short. If he'd heard some kind of noise, it had been subconsciously. He paused now and waited for a count of twenty. When he got to eighteen he heard a noise inside his room.

Sliding the key in the lock would alert whoever was in his room. With silent apologies to the management he braced himself against the wall on the other side, and then launched himself at the door. His heel struck the door just below the doorknob, and wood shattered as the door flew open.

The light from the hall did little to illuminate the room, and he was at more of a disadvantage because the man inside already had his night vision. Clint drew his gun and went in low. The first muzzle flash showed him where the man was, and the second flash was the man's gun discharging into the ceiling as Clint's shot hit him.

The shot flung the man backward and as he hit the window the glass gave and he flew out into midair. He and the glass crashed to the street together. Clint took a moment to light the lamp in the room and then walked to the street. Several people had gathered around the fallen man.

"Somebody call the sheriff, please?"

A man looked up and said, "What for? He ain't good for shit!"

Clint grinned at that and said, "Just call him for me, all right?" and turned to regard his ransacked room.

Sheriff Masters was in his office when he heard the shots, and he knew what they meant. He took out a big red bandanna and wiped his brow, but it didn't help. He was so nervous there was just no way to control the perspiration that was flowing down over his face and under his arms.

Suddenly, he became aware of his own smell, and he knew what it was.

The smell of fear.

There was another man in town who could also smell his own fear, and it didn't please him.

The bartender at the saloon called a man over and asked him to cover the bar for him.

"You're coming back to lock up, ain't ya?" the man asked.

"Yeah, sure," the bartender lied, "I'll be back."

He hurried into the back room, discarded his apron, and then ran out the back door. He grabbed the first horse he saw and rode hell-bent-for-leather out of town.

He knew damn well that Jim Fogarty was no match for Clint Adams, and now the Gunsmith would be looking for *him*.

FIVE

"You lied to me!" Clint said to the sheriff.

"What? What?" the sheriff asked, nervously. "What do you mean?"

"I asked you if you knew Sadler or Leggett."

"So?"

"You said no."

"I *don't* know them," the sheriff insisted.

"Somebody knew I was looking for Leggett," Clint said. "Somebody thought there was something in this room, maybe something that Phil Sadler gave me. Who did you tell?"

"Nobody!" the sheriff said, his voice squeaking. "I didn't tell nobody!"

"Let's try something else."

"What?"

"The man I killed. Do you know who he was?"

"Sure," the sheriff said, apparently relieved to be able to answer a question. "His name was Fogarty, Jim Fogarty."

"Who was he?"

"Just a fella who hangs around town."

"What did he do?"

"Nothing."

"How did he eat, where did he sleep?"

"I only know him from around town," Masters said. "I don't know all that other stuff."

"How long's he been here?"

"About a week, maybe ten days."

"Did you talk to him when he got here?"

"What for?"

"He was a stranger in your town!"

"I don't talk to all the strangers who come into town."

Clint glared at the man for a moment, resisting the impulse to rip the badge off his chest.

"You're a piss-poor excuse for a sheriff, do you know that?"

"Yeah, I—no—hey—"

Clint walked past the sheriff out of the room.

He had just remembered the sweating bartender.

Clint Adams entered the saloon, pushing through a crowd of men who had gathered in front trying to see what had happened down the street.

He headed for the saloon but lost some steam when he saw that there was a different bartender.

"Where's the bartender?" he asked.

"I'm the bartender," the little man behind the bar said.

Clint reached across the bar and took hold of the man's shirt front.

"The other bartender! Where is he?"

"H-he went out the back door. He asked me to watch the bar for a while. I didn't do nothing!"

He released the frightened man and went through the doorway into the back. He saw an apron on the floor and went to the back door. Outside he couldn't see anyone and he was sure the man had run at the sound of the shots.

"Damn!" he said. If he'd only become suspicious when the man had tried to keep him at the saloon longer. Now he was stuck with a no-good sheriff who seemed afraid of him but was apparently more afraid of someone else.

Instead of finding his way around he went back through the saloon and out the front door. He wanted to find the sheriff again.

The body had been removed—probably to the undertaker's—and he asked one of the men who was still milling about where that was.

When he reached the undertaker's there was a light on inside, and he entered. The sheriff turned and stared at him with frightened eyes while another man he'd never seen before simply looked at him.

"Yes?" the undertaker asked.

"I'm here to talk to the sheriff."

"This is Clint Adams, Sam," the lawman said.

"Are you responsible for killing that man?" the undertaker asked. He was about the same age as the sheriff but tall and slim and beardless. His neck had so many wrinkles you would have thought he was a chicken.

"He fired at me first," Clint said. To the sheriff he said, "I have a message for whoever you're working for."

"I'm working for the town . . ." the sheriff said, casting a nervous glance at Sam the undertaker.

"Don't blow anymore smoke my way, Sheriff," Clint said, "I'm not in the mood. Tell your boss not to get in my way. I'm going to find Harrison Leggett, whoever he is, and then I'm going to get some answers." He pointed his index finger at the man and said, "Pass that message along, Sheriff, and then pack your bags."

"P-pack my b-bags?" Masters said.

"That's right," Clint said. "You won't want to be here the next time I ride through."

"W-when will t-that be?"

"I haven't the faintest idea," Clint said, and turned and left.

SIX

Clint went back to the hotel and arranged with the manager for another room.

"Of course," the man said, "we will have to charge you for the damage you did to the door and window."

"I didn't damage the window," Clint said, "the other man did."

"Yes . . . but you shot him."

"Right," Clint said, "I did, after he got into my room. How did he do that, friend? Walk right past your clerk? Or did he bribe him?"

"We don't take bribes!"

"You collect for the window from the other man," Clint said, poking the man in the chest.

"But—but he's dead."

"That's your problem."

"What about the door?" the manager asked as Clint walked away.

"I might pay for that," Clint said, "or I might take it out of your hide."

"M-my hide?"

"That man could have killed me," Clint said, "in

your hotel. Who would have paid for that?"

"I—I—"

"Let me sleep on my decision," Clint said. "Good night."

Clint had removed his boots and shirt when there was a knock on his door. The manager, he wondered? He opened the door and found Reena standing in the hall, a shawl around her shoulders.

"Reena," he said, "this is a surprise."

"It is?" she said. "I knew it. I'll go—" she started away and he reached for her, putting his hand on her arm to stop her.

"Wait! What's the matter?"

"My sister," Reena said, saying the words as if they pained her, "she said you—you wanted me. I should have known better than to—to believe—oh, I'm so embarrassed!"

"No, no," he said, "don't be embarrassed. I just didn't expect you so soon, is all."

"You mean—"

"Come on, come in—if you don't mind being in a man's room after dark."

"N-no, I don't mind."

Reena stepped into the room, and Clint closed the door behind her.

"My sister is always doing things like that to me," she said.

"What?"

"Lying to embarrass me."

"What did she tell you?"

"That you—you liked fat girls."

Clint suspected as much. Rachel, having been rejected, had sent her sister over here to be humiliated. Well, Clint was going to make sure that she wasn't.

"I didn't tell her that."

Reena lowered her eyes and said softly, "I know."

"She asked me to take her to my room," he said, "and I told her no."

Reena's eyes widened and she said, "No man has ever told Rachel no."

"Has she had a lot of men?"

"If Momma only knew," Reena said. "Rachel is always going to men's rooms."

"And you?"

"I—I don't—I'm not like Rachel."

"No, you're not," he said, "you're much nicer. That's why I told her I liked you best."

Reena looked at Clint and then raised her eyebrows. He could see that she didn't know quite how to react.

"I can't believe . . ." she said, "You did? You actually told her that?"

"I did."

"She must have been furious." Reena looked stunned. "I—I don't know what to say."

"There's nothing to say," he said. "Come on, sit down."

There was nowhere to sit but the bed, and she sat on it gingerly.

"Reena, if you're nervous maybe you'd better—"

"No," she said, "I am nervous, but it's not about being in a man's room—your room. You make me nervous."

"I do?" he asked, sitting next to her. "Why?"

"Because you're . . . attractive and nice . . . and you honestly make me feel that you . . . you like me."

He smiled, leaned over, and kissed her. She had soft, full lips. When he kissed her she gasped, and touched her lips.

"I do like you."

"No man's ever told me that before."

"Have you ever been kissed before?" he asked.

"Well, yes, when I was younger. You see, I—developed earlier than Rachel, and when we were younger, boys came to see me. They were . . ."

"Intrigued? Curious about your—your developments?"

"Yes. They used to kiss me, and try to—to touch me, but I wouldn't let them. Then one summer Rachel blossomed. After that they came to see her, to kiss her and to—touch her . . . and she'd let them."

"She never got caught?"

"Well, only once, but it was me who caught her. She was in the storeroom with—with a grown man, and she was—was sucking on him—um, do you know what I mean?"

"Yes, I know. How old was she?"

"Fifteen. I was so—so ashamed."

"She's the one who should have been ashamed."

"She's never ashamed of anything she does."

He reached out and took her hand.

"Reena, there's no reason for you to be ashamed of anything, either."

"I—I'm ashamed of how I am. Fat, I mean. I try to lose weight, but I can't—"

"You're not fat, exactly," he said. "I mean, your mother—I'm sorry—" he said, catching himself.

"Don't be," she said. "I know Momma's fat."

"You're mother is—sloppy fat, Reena," he said, not knowing how else to put it. "You, on the other hand, look very firm."

"Well, firm or not, I'm still fat."

"There are men who like full-figured women."

She laughed without humor and said, "That's what Momma keeps telling me, but I haven't found one yet. You know, I've never—"

"Never what?"

"Never mind," she said, lowering her eyes.

He brought the hand he was holding to his lips and kissed it.

"Never been made love to?"

He kissed it again and she looked at him and nodded, biting her bottom lip. He leaned over and kissed her again, this time longer. Her lips were tight against his, and then they softened as she relaxed. The kiss was almost chaste, but it was the longest kiss she'd ever had and it made her breathless.

"Oh, my," she said, licking her lips. "Mr. Adams, I don't think—"

"Do you want to leave?"

"N-no."

"Do you want me to stop?"

"Are you—you're not going to—"

"Yes," he said, "I am going to make love to you."

"No," she said, "you don't have to. You're not obliged . . ."

"I like you, Reena," he said. "I want to make love to you."

She didn't know what to say.

"Do you want me to?"

She opened her mouth, but no sound came out. She tried again and whispered, "Oh, yes."

SEVEN

He kissed her again, putting his arm around her and holding her close. He found it unusual that such a big girl was not wearing a corset, but he was right when he told her she was firm. Her lips were sweet, and using his own, he pried them open and let his tongue slide into her mouth. She moaned and pressed herself against him. Still kissing her he slid the shawl from her shoulders and undid the buttons at the back of her dress.

"Come on," he said, "let's get this off you."

"You might change your mind if you do," she said, warning him.

"No," he said, "I won't. Trust me."

"I do."

He undid her dress and pulled it down to her waist and left it there for the time being. He wanted to free her breasts because he was curious about them.

"Ready?" he asked.

"I'm ready, Clint."

When they were revealed her first reaction was to cross her arms over them, but she stopped herself and

31

permitted him to look at her.

"Oh, Reena," he said, "they're beautiful."

"Clint, look—"

"No, I mean it," he said. He took one breast in each hand and she bit her lip. "They're round and firm, and the skin is so smooth. And your nipples, they're a lovely pink."

He flicked his thumbs over her nipples, and she moaned and closed her hands into fists, gathering the bedclothes.

Clint found himself growing excited. She truly did have lovely breasts, and he felt an erection growing rapidly.

He slid off the bed to his knees and said, "Let's get this all the way off."

She lifted her buttocks so he could slide the dress off, and then her underclothes, and then she was totally naked. She had a round belly, but it, too, was firm and smooth, and she smelled wonderful.

When he told her that she said, "I like to be clean."

"That's it," he said, "you smell clean."

He leaned into her breasts so that his nose was between them and inhaled. She smelled of soap, but she had started to perspire from nervousness and he could smell her natural scent, as well.

He moved his face across her breasts, touching his nose to her nipples. He kissed her flesh, running first his lips over the smooth surface, and then his tongue. When he touched his tongue to one of her nipples she jumped, and he felt her shudder. He could have sworn she'd had a small orgasm right there. He gathered a nipple deep into his mouth and sucked it, while manipulating the other between his thumb and forefinger. She moaned and arched her back and he put his hands on her waist and then slid them up her back, pulling her tightly to him. He continued to suck and kiss her breasts and nipples until suddenly she shuddered again, this time more violently, and cried out.

"God, what was that?" she asked, and he patiently explained to her that she had experienced an orgasm.

"I can't believe it," she said. "It was wonderful."

"It's only the beginning," he said, and kissed her again. This time when he opened her mouth she boldly thrust her tongue into his and he sucked it.

Breathless, after the kiss she said, "What about you?"

"What about me?"

Unitl now her hands had been firmly pressed down on the bed, but now she picked up her hands and ran them over his naked chest.

"Aren't you going to undress?"

"Do you want me to?"

"Oh, yes."

He stood up and undressed in front of her. She watched, wide eyed, as his penis came into view, erect and throbbing.

When he was naked in front of her she breathed, "God, I've never—I didn't know it would be so—so beautiful." She looked at him hopefully and asked, "Can I touch it?"

"Sure," he said, "it won't bite you."

He stood before her as she studied him, as if trying to figure out how to approach him. Finally, she just leaned forward and closed one hand over him.

"Am I hurting you?"

"No."

Slowly, she ran her hand up and down him, and with her other hand she gingerly felt his balls.

"You're so warm," she said, "the skin is like glass." She looked up at him sharply and asked, "Can I . . . kiss you?"

"You can do whatever you like, Reena," he said. "We have all night."

She used her lips and hands to explore him, and as the minutes went by she became more and more bold. Finally, she opened her mouth and allowed the head of his cock to slide between her lips. She closed her eyes and took more of him inside, and then began to bob her head. Clint guessed that this was what she had probably seen her sister doing when she was only fifteen. Then it had seemed wrong, but now it was so very right.

He reached down and gently took hold of her head, guiding her to the right tempo. His hips began to move as her lips slid up and down him, and then he said, "Stop."

"Mmmm," she moaned as he slid out of her mouth. "Why?"

"Because there's more," he said.

He pushed her down onto her back and got on his knees in front of her. He spread her legs and began to lick her.

"Oh my God, what are you doing?"

"Relax" he said, "open yourself up to me."

She did so, spreading her legs wide, and he lifted them and put one over each shoulder. He leaned into her and began to kiss the flesh of her inner thighs, running his tongue over them, and then licking her vagina in earnest. He pushed his tongue inside of her and she shuddered, moaning. When his tongue found her clit and flicked at it she began to thrash around, and when he sucked her clit into his mouth, she moaned, shuddered, and cried out loud.

"I'm sorry," she said, breathlessly as he joined her on the bed, "I couldn't help it. I can't control—"

"It's all right," he said, kissing her. "It's all right."

"My God, Clint, this has been . . . marvelous."

"It's not over yet," he whispered into her ear.

"I know," she said, kissing his neck. "Please, let's do it now?"

"Yes," he said, sliding atop her. "Yes."

He probed at her with the head of his penis and found her moist and ready. He slid into her easily, encountered her hymen, and pushed gently until finally he broke through.

"Oh!" she cried, jumping as he entered her to the hilt.

"All right?" he said.

"Yes," she said. "Oh, yes, wonderful. You fill me up!"

He slid his hands beneath her and took her big, firm buttocks in his hands, and started to take her in long, easy strokes.

"Mmm," she moaned. "Oh, Clint, yes, oh, yes . . . !"

He went slowly with her, building the tempo easily until finally he was slamming into her and she was holding him tightly to her, moaning and crying and coming and coming, and then he exploded into her and she screamed . . .

Seconds later she said cautiously, "Do you think anyone heard me?"

He looked down at her and asked, "Do you care?"

"No," she said, "oh, no."

She took hold of his head, pulled him facedown to her and kissed him, a hard, deep, probing kiss. "I don't care one bit!"

Clint enjoyed himself.

It had started out as something to do for her, to boost her confidence. It has also been his way of making sure her *sister* was the one to be embarrassed, not her.

At times it felt as if he were in bed with acres of opulent, fragrant flesh. He ran his hands over her, his mouth, his tongue. She was soft yet firm, smooth and warm and sweet, and she was willing and eager to learn all she could learn in one night.

And so it ended up being for him as much as for her.

"Rachel will never believe me."

"No, I don't guess she will," he said, lying beside her. "Do you care about that?"

"Truthfully? No. I thought I would, but as long as I know this night happened, I don't care what she says or thinks. I'm not going to let her bother me anymore."

"Good."

She turned over and put her tongue in his ear, sliding

her hand beneath the sheet and closing it around him. Instantly, he began to swell in her hand.

"Are there other ways . . . to do it?"

"Yes."

"How?"

"Do you want to learn it, and do it, all in one night?" he asked.

"Yes, I do."

"All right," he said. "Put your hands on the bed-post, get on your knees—yes, like that—now stick your big, beautiful butt up in the air."

"Like this?"

"Exactly like that," he said, getting behind her.

"How can you do it like—oh, my God, my God! Oooh, Clint, you're—you're so deep, I feel like you're—you're . . . Oooh . . . yes, yes . . . yes!"

EIGHT

Reluctantly, Reena left before daylight, but she promised to be there when Clint left town.

"Good," he said, because he had a plan to make sure that Rachel knew all about tonight.

Clint slept for a few hours, then rose and had a quick breakfast in the hotel dining room. It was early—though not as early as he'd originally intended to leave—and he was the only diner.

He went to the livery to retrieve Duke and his rig, and then started his exodus from town.

First he stopped at the sheriff's office and went inside. He had to wake the sheriff, who was asleep in a cell.

"Wha–what the . . ." Masters said, coming awake slowly.

"I just want to remind you to give your boss my message," Clint said.

"I told you, Mr. Adams," the sheriff said, rubbing his face, "I don't know—"

"Just tell him."

Clint turned and left. He wondered who would be

so interested in his search for Harrison Leggett.

Could it be Leggett himself who didn't want to be found for some reason?

Then again, the man he'd killed hadn't been sent to his room to kill *him*, but to search the room. He'd only panicked when he was discovered and then fired a shot.

The question was, though, what had he been looking for?

And another question was, who had sent him?

And who was Harrison Leggett?

For that matter, who was Phil Sadler, whose death had started all of this?

All of these questions would probably go un-answered until he got to the town of Pinnacle, and he wasn't going to get there just standing around.

He got his rig going again, but when he reached Rose's Cafe he stopped. True to her word, Reena was outside to see him off. Standing next to her were her mother, and her sister, Rachel, who did not look happy.

Had Reena told her sister where she spent the night?

Clint stopped the rig, got down, and walked over to where Reena was standing. He took the big girl into his arms and kissed her, long and deep, and said good-bye.

As he rode out of town, Rachel turned to her mother and stamped her foot. Her mother turned away from her and walked into the cafe.

As Sheriff Masters had told him, there were several towns between Weston and Pinnacle, but Clint did not stop at any of them. For one thing, he avoided them just in case there was someone waiting to delay him—or search his room again.

He camped off the trail, leaving it up to Duke to warn him if anyone was approaching.

Five days after he left Weston, he rode into Pinnacle, Arizona.

NINE

Pinnacle was quite different from Weston. Where Weston had been a town that had reached its peak in growth, Pinnacle obviously had a ways to go before it reached its "pinnacle."

As he drove down Pinnacle's main street there were signs of its growth all over town. New buildings going up—both wood-frame and brick—and older buildings being repaired. One new building, in particular, had a red, white, and blue banner draped over the entrance, and a sign that said that it would be a theater when it opened.

He kept going until he came to the livery stable, where he turned in his rig, team, and Duke.

"How long you gonna be staying?" the old livery-man asked him.

"I don't know, exactly," Clint said, throwing his saddlebag over his shoulder and taking his rifle from its scabbard.

"Well, I'll need two days in advance, then."

"Here's your advance," Clint said, "and something extra. Take extra good care of that gelding.''

"Sure thing, mister,'' the man said. "He's a good-looking animal.''

"That he is.''

He didn't need directions to the hotel because there had been two of them right on the main street.

"If you're looking for a good hotel—''

"I know,'' Clint said, "there's plenty of them.''

"Stay at the Pinnacle House,'' the man said. "It's the best one.''

"I'll keep that in mind.''

For a moment Clint toyed with the idea of asking the man if he knew Harrison Leggett, but he decided not to reveal himself that way, just yet.

He left the livery and went to the Pinnacle House for no reason other than it was the first hotel he came to.

"A room, sir?'' the clerk asked. He was a young man with a wide gap between his two front teeth which did nothing to discourage him from smiling.

"Yes, thanks.''

"For how long?'' the man asked as Clint signed in.

"I'm not sure,'' he said.

"Well, then, I'm afraid I'll need a little something in advance.''

"Would two days do?''

"That'd be fine.''

Clint paid the man for two days, then accepted his key and went up to his room. He checked the window and found that he overlooked the alley next to the hotel, and not the main street, which was just as well.

It was a sheer drop outside his window, so there was no access for intruders there.

The room was comfortable, with a big bed, a dresser, a straight-backed chair, a pitcher and basin, and a small note on the pillow that told him that bathing facilities were available on each of the hotel's three floors, of which he was on the second.

It was a big hotel in a big town, and he had to find one man and give him a cryptic message from a dead man.

Was that what the man in his room in Weston had been looking for? The message that Phil Sadler had given him for Harrison Leggett? Did they think it was written down, and would they have known it—and known what it meant—even if it was?

Clint sat down on the bed and began to clean his gun. He wanted to make sure it was in perfect working order before he went out on the streets of Pinnacle looking for Harrison Leggett.

After all, the only way he had to find the man was to ask for him.

After Clint went up to his room, the clerk went into the back room where the bookkeeper was working and said, "Jimmy, come out here and stay for a while."

"I'm busy," the older man said.

"I've got an errand to run."

"I got to get these books—"

"Take the damn books out there with you!" the clerk said testily. "I got to go see Old Man Pickard."

At the sound of the name "Pickard," the book-keeper's head snapped up and he said, "Well, why didn't you say so in the first place?"

"Just get your butt out there," the clerk said, and left the hotel by the back door.

"All right," the old man muttered, "but not 'cause you say so . . . ."

TEN

Old Man Pickard sat at his desk and looked out his window, which overlooked the main street. His office was on the second floor of the Pinnacle Bank, as was the Pinnacle Loan Company. Evan Pickard owned both the bank and the loan company, as well as a dozen other businesses in town. An ex-judge who had been off the bench for fourteen years, he had amassed much of his fortune during that time, using methods that might have been termed questionable for a member of the bench.

Evan Pickard liked to think every so often that he owned the town—which of course wasn't true. He merely owned a large part of it.

Pickard stood up and walked to a small sideboard, where he had a decanter of fine French cognac. At sixty-six it was the only vice he still allowed himself. Whores had become useless to him four years ago, and his doctors wouldn't let him smoke cigars anymore. He listened to them because he paid them a lot of money to give him advice like that, and if he went against them it would be like throwing money away.

No one ever accused Pickard of throwing money away.

There was a knock on his door then and he called out, "Come in."

It opened and the most beautiful young woman he had ever seen entered.

"Hello, Granddad," she said, smiling. She hurried across the room and kissed him.

"Hello, Elise," he said, hugging her. "My lord, but you get more beautiful every day."

"You tell me that every day, Granddad," the nineteen-year-old said.

"And it's true every day. Your grandmother, rest her soul, was lovely, and your mother even more so, but you combine the best features of both of them, and put both of them to shame."

"Don't say that, Granddad."

"Oh, you know how I mean it," he chided her.

"Yes," she said, taking the glass of cognac from him, "in the nicest way."

She raised the glass to her lips, but he took it from her before she could drink.

Her hair was the color of honey and hung past her shoulders. Her face was oval, dominated by large eyes that were the clearest blue he'd ever seen. She'd been a pretty fourteen-year-old and a lovely sixteen-year-old, but he never would have expected her to be the absolutely breath-taking nineteen that she was. She had to fight off the boys in town with a stick—and the men, as well. It was lucky she had two older brothers to help her—as well as the fact that she was Evan Pickard's granddaughter.

"What can I do for you today, sweetie?" he asked her.

"I saw this absolutely luscious dress—" she began, but he held up his hand for her to stop.

"Say no more," he said. "Just tell Sam Hall's wife that I said to charge it to me."

"Oh, Granddad," she said, clapping her hands together. "You're the best."

There was a knock on the door again and again he called out for whoever it was to come in.

The door opened and the fool clerk, Benny Hicks, came charging into the room.

"He's here, Mr. Pickard, he's here—"

"Benny!" Pickard said forcefully, and Hicks snapped his jaw shut. "You know my granddaughter, Elise?"

"Oh, sure, of course," Benny Hicks said. "Hello, Miss Pickard."

Elise Pickard looked away from Benny Hicks. Hicks was twenty-five, but he'd been in love with Elise ever since she'd been fourteen and he twenty.

"Who's here, Granddad?" she asked.

"No one, honey," he said, standing up. "Why don't you go and buy that dress, hmm? I'd like you to try it on for me tonight when I get home."

"All right, Granddad," she said. He took her by the elbow and steered her to the door.

"Good-bye Elise," Hicks said, even though he knew there was no hope that she'd answer him.

Evan Pickard closed the door behind his granddaughter, then crossed the room to Hicks and gave him a resounding slap on the side of the face. The old man's large hand bounced off Hicks's ear, filling the younger man's head with a painful ringing sound.

"Don't ever come barging into my office shooting off your big mouth!"

"I'm sorry, Mr. Pickard," Hicks said, holding his ear, "but you said to come in—"

"I didn't say for you to come in jawing away, did I?" the old man interrupted. "Look first, lad, I always tell you that. Look first!"

"Yessir."

"Now, he's here, you say?"

"Yes, sir, just like the telegraph message from Weston said. Clint Adams, the Gunsmith, big as life."

"He sign the register that way?"

"Sure did."

"Well, I'll give him that," Pickard said. "He ain't hiding. Staying in the biggest hotel in town and signing in under his real name. What room did you give him?"

"Two-fifteen, over the alley, like you told me."

"All right," Pickard said. "Get back to the hotel before that fool Wisler sees you're gone. Who you got covering the desk for you?"

"Jimmy, the bookkeeper."

"You tell him to keep his mouth shut."

"He will, Mr. Pickard, I guarantee it."

"Don't guarantee me nothing, Hicks," Pickard said. "You ain't man enough."

"Yessir."

"Now get out!"

"Yessir."

Hicks hurried out, and Pickard sat behind his desk and swiveled his chair around so that he could look out the window. Just beneath the lettering on the window that said LOAN COMPANY, he could see Elise crossing the street.

Pickard hated using incompetents like Hicks and that old bookkeeper, but the one gem that had eluded him in Pinnacle was the Pinnacle House Hotel, which was owned by George Wisler. Once he and Wisler's father had been partners, but Pickard had swindled Martin Wisler out of everything and the man had died broke. Now his son owned the hotel and refused to sell. Somehow, the fool thought that he would get revenge for his father someday—but Pickard was here to tell him that "someday" would come when hell froze over, and not a damned day before!

"I'll have that hotel," Pickard said. It was the only thing he hadn't been able to take away from Martin Wisler twenty years ago, and he'd been trying to get it ever since.

And he would.

He had other problems now, though, like the Gunsmith in town looking for Harrison Leggett. He didn't know how Adams knew about Leggett, or why he was looking for him, but he intended to find out.

And if the Gunsmith threatened to get in his way, he would end up the same way Phil Sadler had ended up.

Dead.

ELEVEN

Clint left his hotel and went looking for a place to have dinner. The hotel had a large dining room, but he also wanted to take a turn around town. Maybe he'd get lucky and find Harrison Leggett's name on a window or something. That sure would save him a lot of trouble.

It wasn't to be, though, and he finally settled on a small cafe for dinner. As he entered, he hoped it wouldn't be run by a woman with two daughters. He was relieved when a big man with hairy forearms came out the kitchen to take his order.

When he got the food the taste of it made him wish he was back in Rose's in Weston, daughters or no.

He hastily left the cafe and made a beeline for the nearest saloon. A shot of whiskey would kill anything that might have been in the food.

He had a whiskey and then ordered a beer, and when the bartender came over, he finally asked for Harrison Leggett.

"Who?" the man asked, a blank look on his face.

53

"Harrison Leggett." Clint said again. "You know him?"

"I never heard of him," the man said. He was a big, florid-faced man with a stomach that strained against his white apron. The saloon had the grand name of Jubilation House, although when Clint entered, he didn't see much to be jubilant about. Even the two girls working the place looked like they wished they were someplace else.

"You're sure?"

"You callin' me a liar, mister?"

"No, of course not."

"Or maybe you don't think I got a good memory?"

"Your memory's fine," Clint said. "It's just your manners that need some work."

"You wanna try and improve my manners?" the man asked, belligerently.

"Are you kidding?" Clint asked. "I don't even want to talk to you anymore."

He left his full mug of beer and walked out of the Jubilation House, with no intentions of ever returning.

As he was crossing the street, someone slammed into him coming from the other direction. It was a young woman carrying a box, only the box ended up on the ground in the middle of the street.

"I'm sorry—" he said, even though it had been her fault.

"Oh, my dress," she said, starting to bend over for the box.

"Let me," he said, and leaned over to pick up the box. At that moment he saw the buckboard, whose driver was looking somewhere else. As the two horses pulling it bore down on them he shouted, "Watch out!" and grabbed the young woman's arm, pulling her away with him.

The buckboard scooted by, kicking dust up in their faces.

"That fool!" she cried. "He almost killed us!"

"Are you all right, Miss?"

"Oh, I'm all right, thanks to you," she said. "I'll have to get cleaned up, though."

"Well, even covered with dust you're still the prettiest sight I've seen in some time."

She took a good look at him for the first time and smiling, said, "Why, thank you." It occured to her then that her dress box had been on the ground and she said, "Oh, my dress."

"Right here," he said, holding it up in his hand, safe and sound.

"Oh, thank you," she said. "It's one of a kind, and if it had been ruined—I'm sorry, but you saved my life and I haven't even asked you your name."

"My name is Clint Adams, Miss—"

"Pickard, Elise Pickard."

"A name equally as beautiful as its possessor."

"You have a way with words, don't you?"

"Remarkable-looking women bring that out in me, I guess," he said.

"So I see," she said. "Are you a stranger in town?"

"Just arrived."

"Well, I'd be very pleased if you would join my family and myself for dinner. I know it's short notice— have you had dinner yet?"

"Not so you'd notice," he said, thinking of the

plate he'd left more full than empty at the cafe.

"It is short notice, but if you come I'll—I'll try on this dress and show you what you saved."

"How could I refuse an offer like that?" he asked. "Do I have time to go back to my hotel and clean up?"

"Of course," she said. "My house is that way, at the south end of town. You can't miss it. It's the biggest house in town."

"Now I'm self-conscious about what I have to wear."

"Don't be self-conscious," she said. "You saved my life, and I'm sure my mother and grandfather will welcome you, no matter what you wear."

"In that case, I'll look forward to it. In an hour?"

"An hour would be fine. See you then, Mr. Adams."

He tipped his hat and watched her walk away, then wondered what the hell he was doing accepting dinner invitations from a strange young woman, when he had a man to find.

Oh, well, maybe someone in her family would know who Harrison Legget was.

When Pickard returned home that evening he saw that the table was set for an extra place.

"Why four places?" he asked his daughter, Elizabeth. She had been named for her mother, and when her daughter was born—the last of three children—she decided that she would not also be Elizabeth, so she named her Elise.

"We're having company," Elizabeth Pickard said, taking her father's jacket from him.

"Smells good. What's Annie cooking?"

"Roast chicken," Elizabeth said, "a big one."

"One of the young men who's been chasing Elise around?" he asked. "Or is it one of the older ones?"

"Neither," Elizabeth. "She met a stranger in town today."

Pickard looked sharply at his daughter.

"Is Elise in the habit of inviting strangers to dinner, now?"

"Only when they save her life."

"What?"

Elizabeth told Pickard about the indicent with the buckboard.

"And he was quick enough to save her new dress, as well," she finished.

"Well," Pickard said, "I can see why she would be impressed, then. Who is he?"

"She says he is an older man, but very attractive," Elizabeth said. "His name is Clint Adams. Would you like a drink before dinner?"

She failed to notice the surprised look on her father's face.

"Yes," he said, wonderingly, "yes, I think I need a drink."

TWELVE

When Clint went back to the hotel he decided that since he was having dinner with a lovely young lady — and her folks — he'd make use of the bathing facilities.

Freshly scrubbed and dressed, he walked to the south end of town and sure enough, the girl had been right. He couldn't have missed the house if he tried. It had four columns in front and looked as though it should be on a southern plantation.

With curiosity, he ascended the steps to the front door and knocked, and was admitted by a black man in a white suit.

"Hello," he said. "My name is Clint Adams. I'm invited to dinner."

"Yes, sir," the man said. "Come this way, please. The judge is waiting for you."

"The judge?" Clint said, but the man was already leading the way.

Clint followed him down a short hallway to the large oak door, when the black man knocked. A voice called out "Come in," and the man opened the door and announced Clint.

59

"Clint Adams, sir."

"Bring him in, Julius."

The black man stepped aside and allowed Clint to enter the room.

"Close the door, Julius," the white-haired man behind the desk said.

After the door closed Pickard said, "My name is Evan Pickard."

"Mr. Pickard."

"You're Mr. Adams?"

"Yes."

"Take a seat, please."

Clint sat in a well-stuffed chair with high arms that was placed precisely in front of the man's desk.

"There's a pretty famous fella with the same name," Pickard said. "Clint Adams. They call him the Gunsmith. Would that be you?"

"It might."

"Don't play coy with me, sir. Are you or are you not the Gunsmith?"

"Some people call me that, yes," Clint said. "I don't, as a rule, acknowledge it as a name."

"I see," he said. "Well, considering your reputation, that's probably wise."

"A reputation is little more than a lie that's gained an enormous amount of support."

"I had never looked at it quite that way," Pickard said. "Would you like a cognac?"

"No, thanks."

"Do you know what cognac is?"

"It's not only people with money who drink fine liquor, Mr. Pickard."

"I suppose not," Pickard said, "but I was a simple man for most of my life, Mr. Adams, so I figure I'm allowed to be a snob now that I'm rich."

"I guess you've earned that right."

"You're damned right I have."

"Now that we've agreed on that, can we have dinner?"

"Did you just happen to run into my granddaughter this afternoon, Mr. Adams?"

"As a matter of fact, she ran into me."

"I'm sure it looked that way."

"Didn't your granddaughter tell you how we met?"

"I haven't exactly talked to her about it, but I did talk to her mother. I understand you saved her life."

"Hardly. Just a careless buckboard driver."

"So I understand. I'm gonna find that driver and it's going to be a long time before he gets on another buckboard."

Clint was glad at that moment that he wasn't that buckboard driver.

"When do we eat dinner?" he asked.

"Is that all you expect to get out of this?" Pickard asked. "Dinner?"

"I think I was promised a good dinner."

"And a good one it will be. I have the best cook in the county."

"I'm glad to hear it."

"What are you doing in Pinnacle, Mr. Adams?"

"Passing through."

"On your way to where?"

"Nowhere in particular."

"Well, I suppose after what you did for my granddaughter I should offer you my assistance."

"In what?"

"In anything. You need any help at all while you're in town—or in Arizona—you let me know. I've got a lot of influence."

"I heard your man called you 'Judge'."

"I did have the honor of sitting on the bench," Pickard said, "but that was a long time ago."

"I see. Criminal judge?"

"I handled a variety of matters." The old man finished his cognac and stood up. "I suppose we ought to go in to dinner now."

"Is the interrogation over?"

"Is that what this was?"

"Wasn't it?"

"Yes," Pickard said, after a moment, "I suppose it was. You must understand that Elise has no father and I feel responsible for her safety."

"I guess I can understand that."

Pickard came up alongside Clint, and for a moment Clint thought the old man was going to put his arm around him.

"Let's go in to dinner, Mr. Adams. Can I call you Clint?"

"Sure," Clint said, "why not."

"You can call me Judge."

THIRTEEN

The Judge led Clint to the dining room, where two very lovely women were waiting. Clint noticed the look of surprise on Pickard's face, and he wondered if perhaps Pickard had never realized how beautiful these two women—his daughter and granddaughter—truly were.

Clint had met the granddaughter, Elise, and so was not surprised to see that she was radiant. The other woman, however, was to him equally radiant, if not more so. Elizabeth Pickard was surely in her late thirties, and yet she appeared much younger than that. She must have been very young when she had her daughter.

Elizabeth had the same finely textured hair, the same flawless skin and full bosom, and it would depend on the man you spoke to which of the two was more beautiful.

To Evan Pickard, of course, his daughter was his daughter, and fathers rarely saw their daughters as beautiful, alluring women. Not so with granddaughters, and Pickard thought that Elise was even more beautiful than her mother and grandmother, as he had told her earlier that day.

To Clint, however, there was something about the older woman that the younger woman did not have. There was a poise that comes with age and experience, there was a firmness of body, and an angle of the face that all came with time. Technically speaking, Elise may have been more classically beautiful than her mother, but in Clint's book it was the older woman who commanded his attention.

This seemed to become apparent during dinner to everyone but Pickard himself. He did not notice that most of Clint's conversation was directed at Elizabeth, and he did not notice how this fact seemed to be annoying Elise. She tried to divert Clint's attention away from her mother several times, but each time Clint managed to bring his attention back to the older woman. It was even more annoying to Elise that she was sitting *right beside* Clint, and yet he still favored her mother with most of his attention.

Clint had to give the old man credit for staying away from his interrogation tactics during dinner, but that last statement of Pickard's—about helping Clint with anything at all—made Clint wonder. The man obviously had a lot of clout. In fact, his arm could probably extend to Weston with no problem.

Could it have been Evan Pickard who sent someone to search his room in Weston?

Could it be that Pickard knew Harrison Leggett and/or Phil Sadler?

And if that was the case should he bring up the names—well, certainly not here at dinner-

Or should he?

Maybe springing it at dinner, unexpectedly, would bring out a more honest reaction from everyone.

He decided to give it a try.

"So, it's really nothing in particular that brings you to Pinnacle, Mr. Adams?" Elizabeth Pickard said.

"Clint, please. I thought we settled that."

"All right . . . Clint."

"To answer your question, there is someone in particular I'm looking for while I'm passing through."

"Oh? Who's that?" Elizabeth asked.

"Harrison Leggett."

He watched all three, and if he was expecting some inadvertent admission, he was sorely disappointed.

Pickard was stoic, as if he'd been expecting the name and was determined not to react. He didn't react at all, which was odd. Even if he didn't know Leggett there should have been something—a shrug or a shake of the head—but there was nothing.

His daughter and granddaughter reacted properly. Both frowned, as if trying to place the name, and then professed their ignorance.

"Is he a friend of yours?" Elise asked.

"No, actually he's just a friend of a friend, who asked me to look him up if I was in town. You don't know him, huh?"

"Never heard of him," Pickard said.

"That's a shame," Clint said.

"Maybe you've got the wrong town?"

"Well, that's a possibility, I guess . . ." Cilnt said, and the question of Harrison Leggett never came up again.

Of course, Pickard faded into the background for the rest of the meal, and before dessert was served he excused himself, pleading some pressing work he had in his office.

"I apologize for my father, Clint," Elizabeth said. "He's a very busy man."

"So I understand," Clint said. "Still, I'd much rather spend my time talking to two lovely ladies."

They chatted through dessert, and then Clint announced that he had to leave because it was getting late.

"Well, if my father was the proper host he would have taken you into the den and offered you a cigar and a drink."

"Everything was wonderful, Elizabeth," he said, standing up.

"I'll walk you to the door," Elise said, very quickly. She rushed forward and took his arm.

"Elise will see you out, Clint," Elizabeth said. "Thank you for coming. If you're staying in town a few days, perhaps we can do this again."

"I'd like that," he said.

"Come on," Elise said, steering him out of the dining room.

When they reached the front door, she turned in front of him very quickly, put her arms around his neck, and kissed him, rubbing her body up against him. His reaction was instinctive, and the kiss went on for some time.

"I can come to your room later," she said in a whisper.

"I don't know if that's such a good idea, Elise," he said.

"Why not? Because you're older?"

That had never been a problem with Clint. He'd always felt that as long as the lady was willing, and old enough, it didn't matter about the years between them.

"That's not it."

"My grandfather? You're not afraid of him," she said. "I can tell."

"Not, it's not your grandfather."

She frowned then and backed away from him.

"It's my mother, isn't it?"

"Elise—"

"I saw how you looked at her at dinner," she said, accusingly. "You prefer my mother to me, don't you?"

"It's not that—"

"Why?" she demanded. "She's older, she's not as beautiful as me."

Clint thought about Rachel from Weston, then. There was no shortage of immodest women in his life these days.

"Elise, listen—"

"Never mind," she said. "There's the door, you can let yourself out."

She stormed away from him, and he stood there for a few moments before finally letting himself out.

FOURTEEN

Evan Pickard remained in his office until an hour after Clint Adams had left. At that time his daughter Elizabeth knocked on his door and opened it.

"Father?"

"Yes?"

"That boy from the hotel, Hicks, is here."

"Let him wait," Pickard said. "Come in and close the door, Elizabeth."

She did as he asked.

"Sit down."

"What's wrong?"

"What did you think of that man, Adams?"

"He was very pleasant."

"Attractive?"

"Yes."

"Are you attracted to him?"

She frowned and said, "What are you asking?"

"His name is Clint Adams."

"I know that."

"Otherwise known as the Gunsmith."

"A gunman?"

"That's right," Pickard said, "a killer! I want you to make sure that Elise doesn't see him again."

"How do you expect me to do that?"

"She's your daughter."

"She's nineteen, Father," Elizabeth said. "She's not a child, anymore. I can't lock her in her room, and I can't keep her with me all day."

"Just . . . just do what you can."

"I'll talk to her."

"All right."

Elizabeth opened the door, then turned back to her father and said, "What does he want with Harrison Leggett, Father?"

"What?"

"I asked—"

"I heard you," Pickard said. "I don't know what he wants with him, but I've told you we don't discuss our business with strangers."

"I know, but . . ."

"But what?"

"Maybe you should have the sheriff talk to him—"

"Don't worry yourself about business, Elizabeth— unless you want to become involved in the family business?"

She shook her head and said, "Never mind. I'll send the boy in and say good-night."

"Good-night, Elizabeth."

"Don't stay up too late, Father. You know what the doctor said."

"I know," he said, scowling. "Good-night."

She went out and he poured himself a cognac while he waited for Hicks to arrive.

Clint went to the closest saloon—the Cold Cash—and ordered a beer. He thought about Elise Pickard's offer and wondered why he didn't take it. Maybe if it had been her mother making the offer he would have.

This saloon was larger than the one he'd been in earlier, and the bartender was friendlier. There were girls working the room, and a lady dealer at the blackjack table. The other game tables—faro and roulette—were being worked by men.

Clint took his beer and went over to the blackjack table.

The woman appeared to be in her mid-thirties. She had ash-blonde hair that hung straight to her shoulders, darker eyebrows, and her eyes were deep blue. Her mouth was like a slash of crimson on her face, but beneath the harsh lip rouge her lips were full and firm-looking. The heavy makeup she wore was all part of her uniform, like the white silk shirt she was wearing.

She was dealing to two men, and there were two open seats.

"Hi," he said, sitting down.

"Hello," she said without looking at him. She finished dealing to the two men, and he watched her play. She had a six facing up, which meant the most she had was seventeen, if she had an ace underneath. More than likely she'd play the ace as a one, so he figured her for sixteen, which meant she had to hit.

"Hit me," one man said, and she dealt him a queen on top of his five. "Ah," he said, going bust.

"Card," the second man said. She dealt him a seven and he stayed.

She dealt herself a five, flipped over her hole picture card and said, "Dealer has twenty-one."

"Jesus," the second man said, flipping over his hole card to show that he had twenty. "She's amazing."

She looked at Clint now as she raked in their chips and asked, "Are you playing?"

Her bold gaze was like a challenge, and he took out some money and said, "I'm playing."

When Hicks entered his office, Pickard didn't bother offering him any cognac. It would have been a waste of good liquor.

"Hicks, I want some of your friends to pay a call on Clint Adams."

"A call, sir?"

"Yes," Pickard said, "a late night call."

"For what, sir?"

"I'm going to tell you for what, Hicks," Pickard said. "Listen carefully, because I want this done tonight."

Clint played methodically and by the rules. After an hour he was well ahead. The other players at the table came and went, but Clint stayed. He found out that the woman's name was Sandra, and that she hated being called Sandy. He also discovered after sitting there for an hour that she had become very friendly towards him, whereas she was still very businesslike to the other players.

He liked her.

"I've got to take a card, Clint," she said.

"Take it," he said. "It won't help you."

She dealt herself a seven on top of her four, and then turned over her hole picture card.

"Twenty-one," she said. "Sorry."

"Oooh," he said, as if she'd taken a bit out of him. "You look sorry."

He turned over his hole card to show that he had twenty. He wasn't the first one she'd done it to.

"You owe me a drink for that," he said.

"At least," she said, calling one of the girls over. "One now," she added, "and maybe one after work?"

He looked at her, regarding him with her deep blue eyes beneath raised bushy eyebrows. Even with the garish makeup she was a sexy sight.

"Maybe more than one," he said.

"I found him," Harley Race said.

"Where?" Hicks asked.

"He's in the Cold Cash, playing blackjack."

"All right," Hicks said, "get two of the others and wait for him."

"What about you?"

"Me?" Hicks said, looking at the bigger, older man. "What about me?"

"Why don't you come along, Hicks?" Race said,

slapping the smaller man on the back.

"Ow. . . . No, not me. You get two of your friends to go with you."

"Sure, Hicks," Race said, "you just like to give the orders, right?"

"They're the Judge's orders, Race."

"That's right," Race said, poking Hicks in the chest. "And don't you ever think that we don't know that."

"All right, all right," Hicks said, jabbing his chest. "Just get it done, huh?"

"Oh, it'll get done," Race said. "You just have our money."

As Race walked out of the Pinnacle House, Hicks rubbed his chest again and thought that pretty soon Race and all his crude buddies would be bowing and scraping to him the way they did to the Judge.

FIFTEEN

"Who is this fella?" Joe Emerson asked.

"I don't know," Race said.

"Well, what are we supposed to do?" Paul Smith asked.

"We're supposed to detain him, and then I'm gonna ask him a question."

"What question?" Emerson asked.

"Maybe I'll ask him how come he wins at blackjack," Race said, and laughed.

"Blackjack," Clint said, turning over his hold card.

"Your luck is holding," Sandra said, "but time is running out."

"Near closing?"

"Yes," she said, "This'll be the last hand. Want to double your bet?"

Clint was alone at the table with her so he said, "Sure, why not?"

Clint put his bet down and Sandra dealt out the cards. Clint had two sixes, and flipped one over.

"Split," he said, placing a matching bet alongside the second six.

She smiled and dealt him two more cards. A jack fell on the first six giving him sixteen. On the second six she deposited a third.

"Split?" she asked.

"Why not?" he said, and set down his bet.

She dealt him two more cards, a king on the second six, and an ace on the third one.

"Sixteen, sixteen, and seventeen," she said.

"I'll stand."

"On all three?"

"On all three."

"You don't give me much choice," she said, looking down at her seven. She dealt herself a card, an eight, and said, "The dealer goes bust."

"What a way to end a night," Clint said.

She gathered in the cards and said, "Who says the night is over?"

"Here he comes," Race said.

"He ain't alone," Emerson said.

"What do we do now?" Smith asked.

"We do what we're gettin' paid to do," Race said. "Let's go."

"I guess you must be pretty luck at cards," Sandra said to Clint as they left the Cold Cash Saloon together. She had one arm linked in his, and in the other hand she carried a glass of whiskey she'd gotten from behind the bar.

"Sometimes."

"What about with women?" she asked.

"What about them?"

"Are you lucky with women?"

"Sometimes."

"Like tonight."

"Am I lucky tonight?"

"I don't know," she said. "Maybe I'm the lucky one. Where can we go to find out?"

"My room?"

She squeezed his arm and said, "I thought you'd never ask."

Race, Emerson, and Smith took up positions inside the alley that Clint and Sandra would have to pass on the way to the hotel.

"Do we kill him?" Emerson said.

"No," Race said. "Just soften him up a little."

"What about the dealer?" Smith asked, licking his lips. "I been wanting a chance at her for a long time."

"Leave the girl alone," Race said. "We still got to live in this town."

"Yeah, but—"

"Either one of you touches the girl, you'll have to deal with me."

"What is she," Smith grumbled, "your sister?"

As Clint and Sandra passed the alley, Emerson and Smith rushed out and grabbed him, dragging him into the alley. Race came out and grabbed the startled Sandra and pulled her into the dark alley.

"Hey!" she shouted.

Clint was about to shout something himself when

a fist hit him in the stomach, driving the air from his lungs. The men who were holding him were both large and strong and he couldn't pull his arms free.

Race had Sandra by both arms and pushed her deeper into the alley, where she sprawled onto her hands and knees.

"Stay there and you won't get hurt."

"What's going—"

"Shut up!" he said.

It was took dark for her to see anything more than shapes. The huge shape of the man who had pushed her and the shape of Clint and the two men who were holding him and pummeling him.

Likewise, Clint couldn't see a thing because it was dark, and because the men administering a beating to him were holding him bent over so he couldn't get a look at them.

They had done this before.

"That's enough!" Race said.

He walked over to where Emerson and Smith were holding Clint, who hung limply between them. They'd worked on his belly and ribs, and while there was some pain, he was still conscious.

"Can you hear me, friend?"

"I hear you," Clint said, *"friend."*

"Why are you looking for Harrison Leggett?"

"Who?"

The man punched him in the stomach, then waited a few moments until he got his breath back.

"Let's try again," Race said. "Why are you looking for Harrison Leggett?"

"None of your business."

"Make it hard on yourself," Race said. He was about to hit Clint again when there was a shot.

"Ow," one of the men holding Clint shouted, and his left arm was suddenly free. He lashed out at the man still holding him and connected. The blow wasn't truly effective, but it did cause the man to release his right arm, after which Clint dropped to the ground and groped for his gun.

"I'm hit, Race!" Emerson shouted.

"Get out of here!" Race shouted to them.

The man was free and if he drew his gun, someone would get killed. Race didn't have any instructions about killing, so he pushed the others out of the alley ahead of him and followed.

"Are you all right?" Sandra asked, rushing to Clint's side.

"Yeah," he said, breathlessly. "What happened? Who fired?"

"I did," she said. "I always carry a derringer on me when I'm dealing. Some people don't like the hands I deal them."

"Well," he said, holstering his gun. "I don't have any complaints about that."

She helped him to his feet and asked, "Do you want to go find the sheriff?"

"Tomorrow," he said. "Let's just go to my room."

"Boy," she said, "it takes more than a little beating to dampen your spirit, huh?"

"It could have been worse if not for you," he said. "The least I could do is thank you properly."

"I don't have any problems with that," she said.

SIXTEEN

"Pour a couple of drinks," Clint said as they entered his room. "We deserve them."

He lit the lamp while she found two glasses and poured two drinks.

"Look at that," she said, looking at her knees, which were covered with dirt.

"Sit down," he said, "I'll clean them."

"What about you?" she asked, handing him a glass. "You're the one who got beat up."

"I'm all right," he said. "A little sore, but all right."

"Well," she said, slipping off her boots and wiggling her toes, "you take care of me and I'll take care of you."

He got the pitcher and basin from the dresser, and a towel, and then knelt in front of her, putting his drink on the floor. He wet the towel and cleaned her knees which were, by the way, excellent.

"They're not scraped," he said.

"Well, that's good."

He saw that she was wiggling her toes.

"How are your feet?"

"They're fine," she said, "I've just been on my feet a long time."

"Give them here," he said. He lifted one foot onto his knee and washed it, massaging it at the same time.

"Ooh, that feels good," she said as he rubbed the bottom of her foot.

He picked the other one up and did the same.

"How's that?" he asked.

"Wonderful," she said, lying on her back. "Give me a moment and I'll tend to your wounds."

"You want to spend the night?" he asked.

"I don't think I could leave if I wanted to."

"Well, let me get the rest of your clothes."

He undid the belt and pulled off her skirt, then unbuttoned her shirt and, with her help, got it off. She lay there in her underwear, and he admired her firm body.

"Can I have that towel?" she asked.

"Sure."

She took it and used it to clean all the makeup off her face.

"You just took off five years," he said.

"The makeup makes me look older, harder," she said. "It comes in handy when you're dealing blackjack to drunks."

"How old are you?"

"Twenty-six."

"Move up on the bed," he said. "Here, lift your hips." He pulled the bed clothes down so that she was lying on the cool sheet.

"Mmm," she said. "You wanna get married?"

"Not right now."

"Hmm," she said, her eyes closed, "maybe later, all right?"

"All right."

"Just give me a minute . . ." she said.

"Yeah, I know," he said, "and you'll tend to my wounds," but she didn't hear him.

She was asleep.

He covered her, admiring her face in repose. Even asleep that face exuded sex. She was one of the most sensuous women he'd ever met, without being classically beautiful.

He returned the pitcher, basin, and towel to the dresser and poured himself another drink. He then removed his shirt and checked his condition. He was sore and he'd have some bruises, but there would be no lasting damage.

He took his drink to the window and looked out at the dark alley where, just moments ago, he had been helpless. It had not been a pleasant feeling, and someone was going to pay.

He'd mentioned Harrison Leggett's name to four people. The bartender at the saloon he'd gone to earlier, and then to Evan Pickard, his daughter, and his granddaughter.

He doubted that the bartender would have had any reason to send three men after him. He might believe that Elise had sent them to beat him up—she'd been angry enough—except that they'd asked about Leggett.

It had to be Pickard who sent them after him.

He finished his drink and toyed with the idea of

another, but he was tired. He propped the straight-backed chair against the door, wedging in beneath the doorknob, and removed his pants and slid into bed next to Sandra. His gun he hung on the bedpost within easy reach. He pressed himself against her, enjoying the feel of her warm, firm flesh, and she moaned and lifted her leg over him.

In bed with a sexy, desireable woman whom he had not yet made love to, and he was going to sleep?

He must be getting old.

"You what?" Hicks asked.

"I shouldn't even be here, since he's got a room in the hotel," Race said, whispering.

"Come back here," Hicks said, drawing Race into the back room. "What happened?"

"I told you," Race said. "He got away."

"How?"

"He had a girl with him and the bitch had a gun," Race said.

"What girl?"

"The blackjack dealer from the Cold Cash."

"You got run off by a little girl with a little gun?" Hicks said.

"Look, Hicks," Race said, poking Hicks in the chest hard enough to make the man wince, "I got a man with a bullet in his arm. You want to tell him he shouldn't have run?"

"No, but—"

"You tell the Judge that if he still wants the job done, it'll get done, but he'll have to wait."

"Don't you have anything I can give him?" Hicks asked, not anxious to go to the Judge and tell him that Race and his friends had failed. He knew the Judge would see it as *his* failure. "Did you ask him?"

"I asked him why he was looking for Leggett, but he wasn't answering. Look, who is this guy?"

"That doesn't matter."

"Like hell," Race said. He left the back room and went behind the desk to look at the register.

"Hey, you can't—" Hicks said, but Race wasn't listening.

He opened the register and turned to the latest entries and read the name of the man he'd beaten up in the alley.

"What the—" he said. He turned and pinned Hicks with a murderous gaze. "You sent me after the god-dam Gunsmith and didn't tell me?"

"I didn't think—"

Race took hold of Hicks by the neck and lifted him so that the man had to stand on his toes to keep from strangling.

"You tell the Judge the price has gone up," he said, tightly. "You got that?"

"Urgh," Hicks said, his face turning red.

"And don't ever pull something like this on me again, Hicks," Race said, putting his face right up against Hicks. "Understand?"

"Urgh," Hicks said again, trying to nod.

Race released Hicks, and the smaller man staggered and leaned against the wall.

"I'll see you later," Race said, slapping Hicks on

the cheek gently and then leaving.

"You'll pay for this," Hicks said, rubbing his throat.

Thoughts of his revenge against Race faded, however, as he tried to think of a way to tell the Judge that what he wanted done had not gotten done.

SEVENTEEN

Clint woke the next morning with something tickling his nose. He opened his eyes and found himself looking at the back of someone's blonde head. It was her hair that had been tickling his nose.

Sometime during the night he had turned over and fitted himself spoon fashion to Sandra's back. Also, sometime during the night Sandra had removed all of her underclothes so that she was totally naked. Clint lifted his hips and slid his shorts off, then pressed himself back against the girl's firm buttocks. His erect penis fit itself right into the cleft between her buttocks. He slid a hand around her and cupped her left breast in his hand. It was firm and warm, and the nipple felt hard against his palm.

"You minx," he said into her hair, "you're awake."

He heard a giggle muffled by a pillow.

"How could I sleep with that . . . that thing pressing against my backside? I was going to give you five more minutes and then I was going to reach into your shorts—"

"You don't have to do that now," he said.

"No," she said, "I see that I don't."

She started to turn over and he said, "No, no, no," and stopped her.

"What's wrong?"

"I like it like this," he said.

He moved her hair away so that the back of her neck was exposed and then kissed her. He moved his lips from her neck to the area between her neck and shoulder, and then to the shoulder itself, and then back again all the way to the other side. At the same time he took her nipple between his fingers and rolled it.

Sandra moaned and reached behind them to take hold of his penis. She opened her legs and slid him between her thighs, then closed her legs over him, and began to roll him between her thighs.

Clint moved closer to her still, pushing his penis beyond her thighs until it was poking at her where she was already wet and waiting. She moved back against him and suddenly the swollen head of his penis was inside of her.

"Mmmm," she said, "that's nice."

They arched together and then a good portion of him was buried inside of her. They began to move together, finding the right tempo, and she was moaning and groaning as he slid in and out of her, still rolling her nipples and kissing her neck.

"Oh lordy!" she said, quickening her pace, and suddenly she was quivering against him.

"Ooh," she said, "what a way to wake up."

He slid his penis out of her, even though he hadn't

yet come. He slid beneath the covers, craning his neck, and licked her vagina.

"Mmmm," she said. "You're gonna hurt your neck. Here." She tossed the sheet off the bed and he slid farther down until he was nestled comfortably between her legs.

She was very wet, and he licked it all up while she moaned and pressed her buttocks into the mattress. He rolled his tongue up and slid it into her. She started writhing and reached for his head.

"Oh, yes, that's it," she said, as his tongue found her clit. She began to rotate her hips as he licked and sucked her, and then she closed her thighs over him as her orgasm gripped her.

"Come," she said, reaching for him, "come up here, you . . ."

He slid atop her and kissed her. She used her tongue to lick his face dry of her, then kissed him and thrust her tongue into his mouth. She clapsed his buttocks tightly and he lifted his hips so that he could slide into her.

"Umm," she said, "oh, yes . . ."

He slid his hands beneath her, cupped her buttocks, and began to slam into her.

"Harder," she cried into his ear. "Oh harder . . . faster . . . damn, yes, yes . . . oh, damn you, that's it . . . that's it . . ."

Finally he felt the rush in his thighs and his loins and then he exploded into her . . .

As they dressed he said, "I don't even know your last name."

"Stone," she said, "Sandra Stone."

"Sandra, about last night—"

"What did those guys want?" she asked.

"I've been asking for a man," he said, "Does the name Harrison Leggett mean anything to you?"

"Leggett?" she said, frowning. "No, I can't say that it does. Why are you looking for him?"

"Well, that's what those fellas wanted to know last night. I can't really say, right now."

"That's okay," she said, "I understand."

"Did you recognize those men?"

"It was too dark. They were big, though, and there's a lot of big men in this town. I guess they won't be easy to find, huh?"

"Maybe not so hard," he said.

"Why's that?"

"You hit one of them."

She had been seated on the bed, sliding on her boots, and she stopped and stared at him.

"I did?"

"Yup."

"Jesus," she said, "I've never shot anyone before."

"Well, you picked a good time for your first, as far as I'm concerned."

"Did I kill him?"

"I doubt it."

"Well, that's a relief," she said. "I don't like the idea of killing anyone."

She pulled on her second boot and stood up.

"Can I buy you breakfast?" he asked.

"You don't have to."

"I want to," he said. "Besides, I'm a stranger and you'll know where to get a good breakfast."

She smiled and said, "You're very honest, aren't you?"

"I try to be."

"And very nice—and very good in bed," she said. "Hmm, in fact, marvelous in bed. Are you sure you don't want to get married and take me away from all of this?"

He smiled and said, "Why don't we discuss that over breakfast?"

EIGHTEEN

Sandra took Clint to a cafe that was at the opposite end of town from the one he'd tried yesterday. Everything about it was nicer—and cleaner—and the food clearly superior.

"Where did you eat yesterday?" she asked.

"I had lunch at a cafe on the other side of town."

She made a face and said, "That's Bud's. He's a pig."

"So I noticed."

"And dinner?"

"I had dinner with the Pickard family."

Her eyebrows went up.

"You were invited by the Judge?"

"No, by his granddaughter."

"Miss Priss-Miss?" she said. "When did you meet her?"

"Yesterday. We bumped into each other on the street," he said, and went on to explain about the near-miss with the buckboard.

"Watch out for those two," Sandra said.

"Which two?"

93

"Mother and daughter," she said. "Between them they'll eat you alive." She reached across the table, touched his arm, and added, "That's a pleasure I'd like to save for myself."

After breakfast Clint asked Sandra to go with him to the sheriff.

"Do you know him?"

"I know him," she said. Something in her voice said that she knew him very well, but Clint didn't ask. "I'll take you over there."

They left the cafe and Sandra led the way to the sheriff's office.

"His name's Dan Haskell," she said.

"How long has he been sheriff?"

"A couple of years."

"How old a man is he?"

"About thirty-two . . . I guess." Again, the tone of her voice told him that it was more than just a guess.

When they reached the office, she opened the door and walked in ahead of Clint. The man seated at the desk fit her description, and he wore a sheriff's star on his chest. His face brightened when he saw her, and he was half out of his chair before he noticed Clint.

"Sandra," he said, straightening up the rest of the way.

"Dan, this is Clint Adams. He got into town yesterday, and last night three men tried to beat him up in the alley near his hotel."

Clint wished he had told Sandra to let him do the talking, but it was too late now.

"Mr. Adams," the sheriff said, sizing Clint up. It had to be obvious to him—from the fact that Sandra was still dressed in her dealer's outfit, and also from the wrinkled conditon of those clothes—that she had spent the night with Clint.

"What brings you to Pinnacle?"

"There's something else I should tell you, Dan," Sandra said, interrupting him.

"What's that?"

"The three men who attacked him? I shot one of them."

He stared at her for a few beats and then said, "Kill him?"

"No," Clint said. "Winged him, I think. Actually, they attacked both of us—"

"Why didn't you tell me that?" Haskell demanded of Sandra.

"It wasn't important, Dan. All they did was push me down."

"Did you get a look at them?"

"No," she said, "it was too dark. Do you want to put me in a cell?"

"Don't be ridiculous."

"Then I think I'll go home," she said. She turned to Clint and said, "See you later?"

"Sure." Aware that Haskell was watching them carefully he added, "I haven't won all I intend to, yet."

"Your luck may not hold."

"We'll see."

She touched his arm in an intimate way and left

without another word to the sheriff.

Haskell walked to the window and looked outside, following her progress.

"What's your connection with her?" Haskell asked.

"I met her last night, playing blackjack."

"Just last night?" Haskell asked, looking at Clint in surprise.

"That's right," Clint said. "Look, Sheriff, if I've stepped into something, let me know—"

"Nah," Haskell said, his tone resigned as he walked away from the window back to his desk. "*I* stepped in something, Adams . . . It's my own fault." Suddenly, the lawman seemed to become aware that he was talking about his private life to a stranger.

"Tell me, are you the same Clint Adams—"

"I'm the same one."

The sheriff sat down and leaned back in his chair, studying Clint again.

"Take a chair," he invited, then. "What brings you to town?"

"I'm looking for a man."

"Who?"

"Harrison Leggett."

"What do you want with Leggett?" Haskell asked.

"Well, I want to—wait a minute . . . you know Harrison Leggett?"

"Sure I do."

"Well, that's a surprise."

"Why's that?"

"Nobody else in this town will admit to that."

"Well, that's not unusual."

"Why not? Who is Leggett, anyway?"

"You're looking for him and you don't know who he is?"

"I was asked to look him up by a friend."

"Well, Leggett was an accountant working for Judge Pickard."

"Working for him?" Clint said. "Does that mean that he doesn't anymore?"

"That's right," Haskell said. "He was fired."

"Fired? Why?"

"Rumor has it he was stealing from the Judge."

"Did you arrest him?"

Haskell shook his head.

"The Judge didn't want to press charges."

"Didn't you find that a little odd?" Clint asked. "That an ex-judge wouldn't prosecute a man he caught stealing from him?"

"In this town," Haskell said, "you don't question the Judge's decisions."

"Does he run this town?"

"No, he doesn't run it . . . but he's got a lot of friends here."

"Well, where does he live?"

"I don't know."

"He lives in town, doesn't he?"

"Not anymore," Haskell said. "After the Judge fired him he left town."

"Left town? When?"

"A month back, maybe more."

Clint fidgeted in his chair.

"Sheriff . . . did you see him leave?"

"Well, no, I didn't actually see him ride out, but the Judge said he left."

"I see."

"What's that mean?" Haskell said. "Why did you ask that?"

Having just met the sheriff Clint didn't want to confide in the man just yet, so he told him nothing about Phil Sadler's death. He also didn't expound on the theory he had just formed in his mind.

The theory that maybe the Judge didn't just fire Harrison Leggett.

Maybe he had him killed.

"Well, thanks for your time, Sheriff," Clint said, rising from his chair.

"About last night," the lawman said.

"Yes?" Clint half expected him to ask about Sandra, but he didn't.

"Did you happen to get a look at any of those three men who attacked you and Sandra?"

"No, like she said, it was too dark. If you check with the doctors in town, though, and check to see if anyone was treated for a bullet wound—"

"I know my job, thanks, Adams," Haskell said, cutting him off.

"Sorry, Sheriff," Clint said. "I didn't mean to imply otherwise."

"How long do you intend to stay in town, now that you know Leggett isn't here?" Haskell said.

"I don't know, Sheriff," Clint said. "I guess I'll have to think about that, won't I?"

NINETEEN

Hicks had decided to wait until morning before going to see the Judge with the bad news. He climbed the steps to the second floor above the bank and knocked on the old man's door.

"Come in," the Judge called out.

Hicks entered and had no time to make his report.

"You failed, didn't you?" Pickard asked.

"They failed—" Hicks said.

"Never mind 'they' failed," Pickard said. "This task was left to you, Hicks. Admit to your failure like a man!"

"Yes sir," Hicks said. "I failed."

"Fool!"

Hicks thought the remark was aimed at him, but in reality it was directed by the Judge at himself, for leaving an important task to an incompetent young pup like Hicks.

"Get out."

"Uh, Judge—"

"What is it?"

"My man, he found out that Adams is the Gunsmith," Hicks said. "He says that if you still want the job done, the price has gone up."

"I want the job done, all right," the Judge said, "but I will no longer leave it to lackeys like you."

Hicks didn't know what the word "lackey" meant, but he guessed that it wasn't good.

"Judge—"

"Get out, Hicks. Don't came back here, ever, unless I send for you!"

Hicks's mouth worked a few more times, but he finally left without another word. His whole world seemed to be crumbling before his eyes.

The Judge sat behind his desk, swiveled his chair around, and stared down at Pinnacle's main street.

It was time to call for Lucky.

When Lucas Lucky—who was never called "Lucky Lucas," or "Lucky Luke," by anyone who valued their health—received the telegraph message from Pinnacle, Arizona, he was in the town of Two Forks, which was two days' ride away.

The telegraph message from Judge Pickard told him to be in Pinnacle in one day.

Lucky wasn't afraid of Pickard, but he knew that reaching Pinnacle in one day would mean much more money than reaching there in two.

There was only one thing that Lucas Lucky liked better than hurting people, or killing people—and that was getting paid to do it.

Lucky found his partner, Mitch Morgan, in the saloon playing poker. Morgan was ten years younger than Lucky and had been riding with the older man for three years now, learning all he could. Lucky looked on him the way a teacher looks on a star pupil. Mitch was, in fact, the only person Lucky had ever really liked.

He reminded him of himself.

"Come on," Lucky said.

"After this hand," Morgan said.

Lucky looked at Morgan's hand and saw that he was holding three aces.

"Now, Mitch."

Morgan cast a longing glance at the three aces in his hand, then folded, and picked up his money.

Outside he said to Lucky, "Why do you do things like that?"

"I want to make sure you still want to learn, Mitch," Lucky said. "That you'll still listen to me."

"Yeah, but three aces—"

"Besides," Lucky said, "that fella sitting across from you had a full house."

TWENTY

Clint wasn't quite sure what to do next.

He went to the cafe where he and Sandra had had breakfast and ordered a pot of coffee.

If Harrison Leggett had indeed left town, where had he gone? And if he was gone, was there any point in trying to track him down and give him Phil Sadler's message? Would it even mean anything to him if he wasn't in Pinnacle?

However, Clint had met Judge Evan Pickard, and he did not seem like the kind of man to let someone who was stealing from him go unpunished. If Pickard was the man who'd had Sadler killed, then it made sense to assume that he'd also had Leggett killed, as well, and then told everyone that the man had left town.

The questions that still remained revolved mainly around Sadler. If it was Leggett who was stealing, why was Sadler killed? And why was Sadler going to meet Leggett?

Then again, was Leggett stealing from Pickard, or was that just something else that Pickard had told

Sheriff Haskell and the other townspeople?

The town seemed inclined to try and protect its benefactor, the good Judge Pickard. Even his own daughter and granddaughter had lied about knowing Leggett.

How was Clint going to get anywhere in Pinnacle if everyone had that attitude?

Or did everyone?

The person to pose that question to was Sandra Stone, and Clint was halfway out of his chair before he realized that he didn't know where she lived. He was going to have to wait for her to show up at the saloon for work before he could talk to her.

She had not seemed as in awe of the Pickard family as others in town had. Perhaps there were others, as well, that she knew about.

Clint was going to need all the help he could get if he was going to find out what really happened to Harrison Leggett.

Idly, he wondered about the sheriff. Was he in Pickard's pocket, or was he his own man?

That was something else that he could ask Sandra about.

"You're fired!"

"What?"

"I said you're fired, Hicks!" George Wisler said.

"I don't understand, Mr. Wisler—"

"Sure you do, Benny," Wisler said. He was a steel-haired man in his late forties, with thick arms and the beginnings of a paunch. "I've suspected that you worked for Old Man Pickard, but now I know for sure."

"I don't—"

"I saw you coming out of his office, Benny," George Wisler said. "Not only this morning, but yesterday, as well. Also, I saw you here with Harley Race. I told you to keep him out of my hotel."

"Mr. Wisler, Race is so big, I couldn't—"

"I don't want to hear it anymore, Hicks," Wisler said. "Get out . . . now!"

Hicks glared at Wisler, then had to look away. He came out from behind the desk and started for the front door, then turned and said, "You'll regret this, Wisler. You'll all regret pushing Benny Hicks around."

"Do everybody a favor, Hicks," Wisler said. "Leave town   today!"

"One day," Hicks said, pointing a shaking finger, "one day, I'll own this town," and stormed out.

"That's the day I'll burn it to the ground!" Wisler shouted after him.

It was something George Wisler had thought about more than once, anyway.

TWENTY-ONE

It was after three P.M. when Sandra walked into the Cold Cash Saloon. Clint was seated in the back with a beer and saw her as soon as she entered. She also saw him and, waving to the bartender, went over to sit with him.

"Did you get some sleep?" Clint asked.

"Some, but I kept dreaming about you. Did you think of me today?"

"Often," he said.

"That's good."

"Sandra, was there something between you and Sheriff Haskell, once?"

"Did he tell you that?"

"No, but it wasn't hard to figure out."

"Well," she said, drumming her fingernails on the tabletop, "there was something once, but not for a long time."

"What happened?"

"No one thing," she said, frowning. "He got possessive, started hanging around while I was working,

giving the customers a hard time when they gave me
a hard time.''

"I could see where he would get in the way.''

"I can handle myself fine behind that table,'' she
said, pointing to her blackjack table.

"In a dark alley, too,'' he said.

Her frown went away and she smiled at him.

"And other places?''

"Like bed?''

"Tonight?''

"After work?''

"*Right* after work,'' she said, and started to get up.
He put his hand on hers to stay her.

"What?'' she said. "Can't bear to see me go?''

"Never, but I also have a question.''

"What?''

"Sit down for a minute.''

She sat.

"What do you think of Pickard?''

"The Judge?''

"Yes.''

"I don't like him.''

"Is there anyone else in town who doesn't like
him?''

"George Wisler,'' she said, without hesitation,
"only I'd say that George hates him.''

"Why?''

"Pickard cheated George's father out of his fair
share.''

"Of what?''

"Of this town . . . except for one thing, of course.''

"What's that?''

"The Pinnacle House."

"The hotel I'm staying in?"

"Right. George's father owned it, and now George owns it, and the Judge wants it. He's wanted it for years."

"Haskell told me that Harrison Leggett was Pickard's accountant."

"Who?"

"Leggett," Clint said, "the man I asked you about last night."

"Well, if the sheriff says he was the Judge's accountant, I guess he was."

"But you didn't know him."

"Never heard of him, but then the Judge has a lot of people working for him."

"Is there anyone else in town that who doesn't like Judge Pickard?"

"No. All of the other people in this town worship the ground he walks on—or they act like they do."

"I guess they figure they need him."

"Only to keep the town alive."

"Why don't you like him?"

"He's a dirty old man."

"Did he . . . try something?"

"Not lately. The way I hear it . . . he can't, anymore."

"Were you born in this town?"

"No, but I came here very young and met the Judge while he still had grabby hands."

"How did you meet him?"

"He hired me."

"To do what?"

"To deal blackjack, silly."

"You mean—"

She nodded and said, "He owns the Cold Cash." She stood up and said, "I've got to get my table ready."

"All right."

"When you see George, give him my regards."

"Another old boyfriend?"

"Hardly," she said. "Just the only other person in this town who I have something in common with." She started away, then turned back, and said, "Come and play with me, later."

That was what he called an invitation.

Clint walked over to the hotel wondering why he hadn't met George Wisler before now. If they had met and talked a bit, it might have saved him some trouble.

He entered the hotel and noticed that there was a different man behind the desk today. He also recalled that when he had left the hotel in the morning, there had been no one behind the desk.

"George Wisler?"

The man looked up at him. He had a granite face and hair the color of steel. He also had huge forearms and large hands. Clint seemed to remember that Judge Pickard had large hands, also.

"You want a room?"

"I've got a room."

"In this hotel?"

"In this hotel."

"That pissant Hicks sign you in?"

"He did."

"What did he charge you?"

Clint told him.

"I thought so. In advance?"

"Yes."

"I owe you money," Wisler said. "That little bug overcharged you."

As Wisler was digging for his money Clint said, "Charge it to my room."

"How long you staying?"

"I don't know. That sort of depends on you."

"On me? Why?"

"I'd like to talk to you."

"About what?"

"About Judge Evan Pickard."

Wisler frowned.

"Are you a friend of his?"

"Hell no," Clint said, "I just eat dinner at his house."

"You do?"

"Well, only once."

"If you're not a friend of his, why were you at his house?"

"Because his granddaughter invited me."

"Are you a friend of hers?"

"No."

"This is getting too complicated," Wisler said. "Let me give you your money back."

"Do you know Harrison Leggett?"

"Pickard's accountant? I did."

"I'm looking for him."

"Are you a friend of his?"

"No."

He stared at Clint for a while and then dug into his pocket saying, "Let me give you your money back."

"Look," Clint said, "can we talk somewhere?"

"About what?"

"About Pickard, about Leggett, and about Phil Sadler."

"Sadler," Wisler said hopefully, "is he a friend of yours?"

"He's dead."

He stared at Clint for a few moments, and then said, "Let's go in the back. I think I need a drink."

TWENTY-TWO

Wisler took Clint through the curtain behind the desk and into a back room.

"Where's your clerk?" Clint asked.

"Hicks? I fired him."

"Because he was cheating your guests?"

"Because he was working for Pickard."

Wisler sat down at a scarred wooden desk, opened a bottom drawer and took out a half-empty bottle of whiskey. He groped around and finally came up with two dusty glasses.

He looked at Clint and said sheepishly, "I usually take it right out of the bottle."

"I'm not fancy," Clint said. He took the bottle, opened it and took a swig, then handed it back. It seemed healthier than using one of those glasses.

"Thanks," Wisler said, and took a drink. Then he extended his hand to Clint and said, "George Wisler."

"Clint Adams," Clint said, shaking the man's hand.

"Who sent you over here to talk to me?"

"Who says someone sent me?"

"You'll excuse me, but you haven't gone to every person in this town asking them if they like Old Man Pickard until you came to me."

"Sandra Stone."

"Ah, Miss Stone," Wisler said, and Clint saw a glint in his eye.

"She said you were the only person in this town that she had something in common with."

"She said that, huh?" Wisler said. "Yeah, well, we both don't like Pickard, but that don't keep her from working for him."

"Maybe it's the only job she can get."

"That girl could get a job anywhere in this town. Hell, I've offered her a job working here plenty of times."

"Maybe it's the only job she wants."

"Now that's more like it," Wisler said. He clucked his tongue and said, "I sure wish I could get her to come to work for me, though."

Clint felt sure that this was more than just a business wish.

"Adams, how would you like to try and straighten out everything you told me outside?"

"Let's just say I'm looking for Harrison Leggett, and I'm not convinced that Pickard simply fired him after finding out he was stealing from him—if he was stealing from him."

"You think the old man had him killed?"

"I say I don't think he would have just let him go if Leggett was stealing from him," Clint said.

"Like you said," Wisler said, "if he was stealing from him at all."

"What do you think?"

"I didn't know Leggett well enough to say if he was stealing, but I think you're right about the old man," Wisler said. "I think he killed him. I wouldn't put it past him. If my old man hadn't died, I think the old skinflint would have killed him, too, just to get rid of him."

"Sandra told me something about Pickard swindling your father."

"Yeah, they were partners fourteen years ago. This was just after Pickard left the bench."

"Do you know why he left?"

"Not for sure, but I wouldn't bet against it being one step ahead of a warrant."

"Tell me more about your father."

"Well, when he and Pickard came here fourteen years ago, this wasn't much of a town. They put some money into it, built it up, and then about ten years ago Pickard used some legal loophole to take everything my father and he owned—except this hotel."

"What happened with the hotel?"

Wisler grinned.

"I guess my old man must not have trusted Pickard completely. He bought this place on his own without telling Pickard."

"How did you come to be here?"

"After Pickard swindled my old man I got a telegraph message from him asking me to come."

"Where were you?"

"East, St. Louis. I ran a saloon there. It wasn't something I couldn't give up, so I sold it and came out here."

"And then what?"

"When I got here, my old man was dead."

"How?"

"He had a heart attack," Wisler said, then he sat up straight and said, "Wait a minute. They *told* me he had a heart attack."

"Just like they been telling me that Harrison Leggett left town."

"I'll be a sonofabitch!" Wisler said. "I'll bet that old man killed my father."

"And what about you?"

"Ah, yeah, that's still a possibility, too." Wisler bent over and pulled a shotgun out from beneath the desk. "That's why I keep this handy."

"Then you don't know where Leggett is?"

"If he's alive, he hasn't contacted me, but then we weren't friends."

"How did you know he was Pickard's accountant?"

"The last time Pickard tried to buy this hotel, he had Leggett with him. He said he was his accountant."

"What did Leggett look like?"

"Tall, thin, in his thirties, his hair was thinning in front."

"Did you know a man named Phil Sadler?"

"Sadler? No, never heard of him." He offered Clint the bottle, but he declined and Wisler took another drink.

"Who's this fella Sadler?"

"I don't know."

"Where is he?"

"He's dead," Clint said, "and that's the only thing I know for a fact."

"You don't know who he was?"

Clint shook his head.

"Just that he was headed here to see Harrison Leggett."

"Where did you meet this fella Sadler?"

"On the trail," Clint said. He didn't know why he was telling Wisler things he hadn't told the Sandra or the sheriff, but he found himself liking the other man. "I sat with him until he died."

"That was decent of you."

"I guess. Just before he died he asked me to come here and find Harrison Leggett."

"Well," Wisler said, "Leggett's not here. Whether he's dead or just gone, he's not here, so I guess any obligation you feel toward Sadler is fullfilled."

"Except one," Clint said.

"What's that?"

"I still want to know who killed him," Clint said, standing up.

"Well," Wisler said, also standing, "I don't know how much help I can be to you—if any—but if you need me, just give a holler. I'd sure like to find out if Old Man Pickard killed my father."

"I can appreciate that," Clint said. "I'll keep you informed."

Clint went out into the lobby and Wisler came out and stood behind the desk.

"Hey, Clint," Wisler said.

"Yeah?"

"You wouldn't be looking for a job as a desk clerk, would you?"

Clint grinned and said, "That's a hell of an offer. Let me think about it."

TWENTY-THREE

Outside, Clint paused in front of the hotel and pondered his next move. It would be helpful if he knew where Harrison Leggett lived. He was trying to decide who to ask when he saw someone across the street he recoginzed. He crossed the street diagonally, so he was sure his path would cross with hers.

When he stepped up onto the walk in front of her she stopped, startled.

"Oh, Mr. Adams!" Elizabeth Pickard said.

"Mrs. Pickard," he said. "I'm sorry, I didn't mean to startle you."

"Oh, that's all right," she said. "My mind was just wandering."

"I thought we settled last night that you would call me Clint."

"I'm sorry," she said, "I forgot . . . Clint."

"Have you had dinner yet this evening?"

"Well, no, but my family—"

"Haven't they ever had dinner without you?"

"Well, of course, but . . ." She trailed off and looked over his head. Clint turned and looked and

119

saw the window of the Pickard Loan Company. He assumed that was Judge Pickard's office.

"Has your father told you to stay away from me?" he asked, turning back to her.

"No, why would he tell me a thing like that?"

"I don't know," Clint said, "you tell me. Maybe he thinks I'd be a bad influence on you."

"Mr. Adams—Clint—I am a grown woman, prone to making my own decisions."

"Are you now?"

"Yes, I am," she said, lifting her chin.

"I suppose that means you'll have dinner with me. I've found this wonderful little cafe."

She hesitated a moment, then stiffened her chin and said, "All right."

Clint put his arm out and she took it, smiling up at him.

She was perfectly willing to make small talk at dinner but anytime the conversation got around to her father or his business, she would suddenly become reticent.

"You have a very lovely daughter," Clint said.

"Thank you," she said, "I'm aware of that."

"She's not as lovely as you, though."

"That's flattery, Clint—"

"No," he said, "it's not. Someday perhaps she will be, maybe even more so, but not right now."

"Well," she said, flustered for the moment, "thank you very much."

"She does seem a bit headstrong, though."

"Why would you say that?"

He realized he'd been referring to the incident in the entry hall, after dinner, which of course Elizabeth knew nothing about.

"When she invited me to dinner she simply wouldn't take no for an answer."

"Oh, I see," Elizabeth said. "Yes, she is quite headstrong."

"Does she take after her father in that regard?" he asked.

"No," she said, smiling a small, secretive smile, "she gets that from me, actually."

"I see. How does your father deal with living with two headstrong women?"

"He's quite stubborn himself, I'm afraid."

"And not all that friendly."

"I'm afraid he does not take kindly to strangers."

"Not even when they save his granddaughter's life?"

"Well, he did appreciate that," she said, "but it seems to me that you are a somewhat devious man, Clint?"

"Me?" he said, feigning indignation.

"Last night you were playing down the incident with the buckboard," she said. "Now you're making it sound quite dangerous. I suppose the danger grows and wanes to suit your purposes?"

He laughed.

"All right, I plead guilty, and I apologize."

"Don't, please," she said. "I find you a very interesting man."

"Well, I find you a very interesting lady, Elizabeth . . . and very lovely, as I've said before." He reached across the table to touch her hand and after a moment she slid hers away from his—somewhat reluctantly, he thought. She didn't quite know what to do with the hand after that, and ended up putting it in her lap.

"I really don't think this was a good idea, Clint."

"Why not?" he asked. "We've each just agreed that the other is interesting."

"I don't . . . think it would be wise for us to . . . to start anything."

"I wasn't aware that we were."

"Don't be coy," she said, "it doesn't suit you. You know there is a mutual attraction here. You felt it all last night, just as I did."

"Yes, I did."

"It didn't make Elise happy, you know. She's quite taken with you."

"I'm sorry," he said. "She's quite lovely, but a little young."

"You're a stranger here, and what's more, you're asking questions about my father. I really don't think I should be seeing you."

"Because he said so?"

"No," she said, "because of my loyalty to him."

"I see. Well, I guess I can respect that. Why don't we have some dessert—"

"No," she said, gathering herself together to rise, "I don't think I will. I think I'll just leave you here."

"Whatever you say, Elizabeth."

She stood up and started to leave, then did something that surprised him. She stopped by his chair, leaned over, and kissed him on the mouth. Her tongue darted tantalizingly over his lips for just a half an instant, and then she straightened up.

"It's a pity, really," she said, and then she was gone. He turned and watched her go out the door.

He was inclined to agree . . . really.

TWENTY-FOUR

"We're pushing these animals pretty hard," Mitch Morgan said to Lucky.

"Well, we want to get there pretty fast."

"What difference could one day make?" Morgan asked.

"You don't know the Judge."

"No, I don't," Morgan said. "You always deal with him yourself."

"That's right."

"Why is that?"

"Because that's the way it is," Lucky said. "That's the way it works."

They rode in silence for a while and then Morgan said, "So what's the all-fired hurry?"

"I don't know," Lucky said. "We'll find out when we get there."

Again there was a period of silence before Morgan's next question.

"You ain't afraid of anyone, are you, Lucky?"

Lucky looked over at Morgan and then looked straight ahead again.

"A man who ain't afraid of nothing is a fool, Mitch.

I've told you that before.''

"Sure, sure," Mitch said, "but you ain't afraid of the Judge, are you?"

"No," Lucky said, patiently, "I ain't afraid of the Judge, Mitch."

"Then why do we jump every time he calls?"

"Because we like money, Mitch," Lucky said. "Don't we?"

"Sure we do."

"And he's got a lot of it, don't he?"

"He sure does."

"Then how about you stop asking silly questions and we just ride, huh?"

"Sure, Lucky, sure," Morgan said. "Anything you say."

Lucky had not told Morgan that the Judge's telegraph message this time seemed to have more urgency to it than in the past.

He went over the wording again in his mind:

IMPERATIVE YOU COME AT ONCE. VERY BIG JOB WAITING. EXTRA MONEY IF YOU MAKE IT IN ONE DAY. BE PREPARED TO GO ALL THE WAY.

E.P.

For the Judge to promise extra money, it had to be a very big job, indeed. Also, going all the way meant that Lucky had to be prepared to kill someone.

The Judge was in a sweat this time, and that meant *a lot* of extra money!

TWENTY-FIVE

"Card!" Clint said.

Sandra dealt him a seven. It fell next to his six, and matched the seven he had underneath. Under normal circumstances he would have stood on the thirteen he had, but his luck was still running good.

He looked at her and shook his head, indicating that he did not want another card.

The man on Clint's left had an eight showing and called for a card. Sandra dealt him a picture card, which put him well over.

"Jesus Christ!" he snapped, flipping his hole card over. He'd had another eight underneath. "I can't buy me a break here."

"You should have stood with sixteen," the player on Clint's right said, "or split your cards." He had stayed with a five showing, and Clint felt that he had either fifteen or sixteen.

"Why don't you mind your business!" the man on the left said. He was drunk and called for another drink. The man on Clint's right shrugged at Clint, and they both watched to see what the dealer was going to do.

Sandra dealt herself another card and said, "Dealer has seventeen. Pay eighteen."

Clint flipped his card over to show that he had twenty. The man on his right flipped his to show seventeen. That was a push with the dealer, so he didn't lose, but he didn't win, either.

Sandra gave Clint his winnings and left the other man's bet where it was. She had already taken the chips from the drunken man on Clint's left.

"Bets?"

Clint bet fifty dollars. The man on his right matched the fifty he'd had there for the hand before. The man on his left bet a hundred dollars. His luck was running terribly and he was throwing good money after bad trying to get it back.

She dealt out the cards for a new hand. Clint had a ten in the hole and a queen on top. He had twenty. Sandra was going to need twenty-one to beat him.

He looked at the card of the man on his right and saw that he had an ace showing. The man on his left had a four.

"Cards?" she asked.

"Hit me," said the man on Clint's right. She gave him a king and he stood. With eleven on the table he was in a good position.

"Clint?" she said.

"I'll stay."

"Sir?" she said to the man on his left.

"How come you call him by his name, but you call me 'sir'?" he demanded.

"I know his name, sir, and I don't know yours."

"Oh, yeah Are you sure you two ain't got something going?"

"Card, sir?"

"I'm gonna split these," he said, turning over another four and betting another hundred. "Gimme some nice cards, sweetie."

She dealt him a picture card on each four, which gave him two hands of fourteen.

"Hit me here," he said. She dealt him another picture card, which gave him twenty-four. "Christ! Hit me here."

She put an eight on his other hand, giving him twenty-two. He'd busted on both hands.

"Jesus Christ!"

She dealt herself a card and said, "Dealer is busted."

If the man had sat on his two hands of fourteen he would have won.

"Bets?" she said.

The man on Clint's right stayed with his bet and so did Clint. The drunk on his left bet two hundred dollars. Clint wondered where he was getting the money from. From his clothes he looked like a ranch hand. On the other hand, the man on his right was wearing a white shirt with a black tie, black pants, and a black hat with a silver-dollar band. His black broadcloth jacket was on the chair back behind him.

Suddenly, from behind them a man came and put his hand on the drunk's shoulder.

"Come on, Emmett, before you lose it all."

"I have lost it all," Emmett said. "That there's the last of it."

"Jesus," the other man said, "we was supposed to buy supplies with that money."

"Watch what this here girl gives me now, Walsh,"

Emmett said. "Come on, girlie, deal."

She dealt the cards out. Clint caught an ace in the hole and a king up top.

"Blackjack!" he said, turning the cards over. She added a hundred and fifty dollars to his hundred-dollar bet for his blackjack.

"Jesus," Emmett said, "she's been dealing him hands all night."

"Emmett," the other man, Walsh, warned, but Emmett shrugged him off.

Clint had already won, so he watched the other two men play.

The man on his right was showing a six, and he said, "Hit me."

Sandra dealt him another six.

"Split sixes?" she asked.

"No," he said, "I'll play it as it is."

"Sir?" she said to the man called Emmett.

He had a ten showing and he said, "I'll just leave it the way it is, sweetie."

Sandra had a three showing, and she dealt herself a seven.

"Dealer has twenty," she said, "pay twenty-one."

"Pay me," the man on Clint's right said, showing the nine he had in the hole.

"Goddam it!" Emmett shouted. He flipped his card in disgust to show that he'd had nineteen. "She's a witch! The girl's a magician. She's cheating!"

"If you have a complaint, sir," Sandra said, "please take it up with the owner."

"I'll take it up with you, sweetie," he said, reaching for her.

Clint was about to move when he remembered what Sandra had said about Sheriff Haskell. He sat back to see how she handled herself.

As Emmett leaned across the table to reach for her with both hands, she pulled out her derringer and stuck it underneath his chin.

Emmett froze and his eyes widened.

"Hey," he said, "hey . . ."

Sandra cocked the hammer on the little gun and sweat started pouring off Emmett's face onto the green felt of the table.

"Do you still want to take it up with me?" she asked him pleasantly.

"Come on, Emmett," Walsh said, grabbing his friend around the waist, "we'll tell the boss we got robbed and hope he don't fire us. Come on!"

He yanked and pulled the man off his chair.

"We did get robbed," Emmett said. Now that Sandra's gun wasn't under his chin anymore he got a little braver, but she still had it in her hand.

"What do you mean we . . ." Walsh said, pulling Emmett out the front door.

Sandra looked at Clint and tucked her derringer behind her broad black belt.

"Would you gentlemen like a drink on the house at the bar while I dry the table?"

"Sure," the man to Clint's right said. "What about you?"

"Why not?"

They both got off their chairs and walked to the bar together. On the way the man put his jacket back on. Clint saw that he had a gun in a holster that had been sewn into the inside of the jacket, almost like the one Luke Short wore.

"Sheldon Scott," the man said at the bar, putting his hand out.

"Clint Adams."

"You're having quite a run of luck, Mr. Adams."

"You're not doing too badly, yourself."

"Not as well as you are, I'm afraid."

They accepted whiskey from the bartender and Scott said, "To our little dealer. She's quite a gal, isn't she?"

"That she is."

They drank to her health.

"She sure handled that sodbuster," Scott said.

"Drunks shouldn't play," Clint said.

"And people who can't afford to lose shouldn't play."

"Amen," Clint said.

He took the opportunity to study Scott. He was obviously a professional gambler, and he exhibited all the patience of one. His night had not begun well but he had controlled his betting and then increased it when he started winning.

He appeared to be in his thirties, even though he sported shocking white hair that was barely an inch long. He had broad shoulders and a strong jaw, and had been trying to attract Sandra's attention all evening, with no luck. Clint liked to think that was because of him, and it made him feel pretty good, because Scott was a hell of a good-looking man.

"You and the dealer friends?" he asked Clint suddenly.

Clint looked into the man's blue eyes to see if he meant anything by that, but all he saw was curiosity.

"Don't get me wrong," Scott said, right away, "I know an honest deal when I see one. I'm just nosy."

"We met last night," Clint said.

When he didn't expound on that statement Scott said, "None of my business, huh? Fair enough. How about letting me buy you another?"

"I'll have a beer this time."

"Good idea," Scott said. "Keep our wits about us. Two beers, my friend," he said to the bartender.

The bartender brought the beers.

"You don't live here, do you?" Scott asked.

"Just passing through," Clint said. "I've been here two days."

"Ah," Scott said, "this is my first day. Nice little town. Looks like it's still going to do a lot of growing."

Clint knew that this was Scott's first day in town. With the man's white hair and his size, he would have noticed him before this.

"On your way to anywhere in particular?" Scott asked.

"No."

"You don't talk much, do you?"

"Not to strangers."

"Well," Scott said, nudging him, "can't say as I blame you for that, but after you and I clean this place out at the blackjack table we won't be strangers anymore, will we?"

"I suppose not," Clint said.

"If you gents are ready," the bartender said from

behind them, "the table is opening again."

"I'm ready," Scott said, rubbing his hands together. Clint noticed his hands, then. They looked
like the hands of a man who was not unaccustomed
to hard work.

"Are you ready, Clint?"

"I'm ready, Mr. Scott."

"Hell, man, call me Shell," Scott said. "All my
friends do."

"All right, Shell."

"Come on," Scott said, pushing away from the
bar, "let's go and take that little girl."

Clint watched as the man forged ahead of him to
the table. Scott was almost six four and with his wide,
powerful shoulders, people just seemed to melt out
of his way.

Clint decided to keep a real close eye on Mr. Sheldon Scott for the rest of the night.

TWENTY-SIX

"Remarkable run of luck," Sandra Stone said later. They were in Clint's room, in bed.

"If I didn't know better, I'd say you were dealing me cards."

"And do you know better?"

Clint quoted Sheldon Scott. "I know an honest deal when I see one."

"You're right," she said. "I take my job very seriously. I wouldn't deal cards to my mother."

"Tough lady," he said, running his hand down her bare belly.

"I want to thank you," she said, wriggling her butt with pleasure.

"For what?" he asked. He placed his hand over her pubic mound.

"For not interfering when that drunk made a grab for me."

"You can take care of yourself," he said. "You more than proved that."

His middle finger dipped into her and she stiffened and moaned. She ran her left hand down over his belly until she reacherd his penis, then closed her hand over it.

"What did you think of that other player?" he asked.

"The gambler?" she asked.

"Yes."

"The one with the white hair, blue eyes, and broad shoulders?"

"That's the one."

"I didn't notice him."

He laughed.

"He sure noticed you."

"He's not my type."

"What is your type?"

As her answer she squeezed his penis.

"I'm flattered."

"You should be," she said, turning toward him and pressing herself against him, "I don't sleep with everyone I deal blackjack to."

"I should hope not," he said. "That would be very tiring, wouldn't it?"

She lifted her leg up over him and said, "Let's see how tired we can get."

She climbed atop him, lifted her hips, and reached between them to guide him expertly into her.

As she rode him, Clint reached up and palmed her breasts. They weren't very big, but they were firm and fit nicely into his hands. He thumbed the nipples, and she bit her lip and threw her head back. She pressed her hands down flat on his chest and began to rotate her hips, moaning as she did so. He even enjoyed the way her smooth buttocks felt as they rubbed against his thighs.

"Ohh, yes . . ." she groaned, rotating her hips faster and faster. Clint was moving his own hips, trying to match her tempo, but she was doing most of the work herself. He felt as if her insides were gripping him tightly, trying to suck his orgasm from him.

Trying . . . and finally succeeding!

TWENTY-SEVEN

In the morning, while Clint and Sandra were sleeping with their arms and legs entwined—both thoroughly exhausted and having agreed to a tie—two men rode into town after pushing their horses all night long.

"It's been a while since we were here last," Mitch Morgan said. "I wonder if that pretty blonde is still dealing blackjack at the Cold Cash?"

"She probably doesn't remember you," Lucky said.

"I doubt that," Morgan said. "I won a lot of money the last time we were here."

"And lost it all back, if my memory is correct," Lucky said.

"Yeah, well . . ."

When they reached the livery they found it locked, but that didn't matter to them Lucky dismounted and used a key that the Judge had given him to open the door. After all, Judge Pickard owned the livery stable.

They walked their horses in, unsaddled them, rubbed them down good, and gave them some feed.

"We'll buy new ones when we leave," Lucky said.

"We'll be able to afford good ones, won't we?" Mitch Morgan said.

"That we will."

"We going to the hotel? The Pinnacle House?"

"No," Lucky said, "there's a rooming house at the edge of town. We'll go there."

As they left the livery, Mitch Morgan said, "What do you think this is about, Lucky?"

"No point in wondering, Mitch," Lucky said. "We'll be finding out for sure later on."

Privately, however, Lucky wondered who it was the Judge wanted him to kill. It had to be somebody good for the Judge to offer extra money.

Why wait to find out? After all, the Judge wanted him here as soon as possible, didn't he? And here he was.

"Mitch, go on ahead to the rooming house and get us a room."

"One each?"

"One will do."

"Where you going?"

"I'm gonna go see the Judge."

"You gonna wake him up?"

"If he's asleep," Lucky said, "I'll wake him up. How else am I gonna tell him that we're here?"

"You really ain't afraid of him, are you?"

Lucky looked at Morgan and said, "Just get the room."

When Elizabeth Pickard opened the front door of her house she stopped short when she saw the man standing outside. She had wondered who would be

knocking on the door this early hour. She hadn't expected to see a man in trail clothes who looked as if
he had ridden hard all night. There was still dust all
over his clothes!

"Yes?" she said. She was certain that she did not
know him.

"Mrs. Pickard?"

"Yes."

"I'd like to see the Judge, please."

"At this hour of the morning?" she said. "He's
still asleep!"

"That's all right," the man said, "I'll wait until
you wake him."

"I will not wake him—"

"Mrs. Pickard," the man said, "if you do not wake
him, I assure you he'll be very angry with you. Now,
he asked me to come as soon as possible and I'm
here. I would like him to know that."

"Well, if you'll leave me your name, I'll—"

"Please," he said, "don't force me to announce
myself."

She stared at the man for a few seconds, then decided to let her father deal with him.

"All right, then," she said, "I'll wake him—and
I can assure you that he won't be very happy."

"Thank you."

"What's your name, please?"

"Just tell him Lucky is here."

"Lucky?"

"That's right."

"Wait right there."

"I'm not going anywhere, ma'am."

She closed the door in his face and went upstairs to wake her father.

Evan Pickard came awake slowly.

"Wha-what is it? Elizabeth?"

"I'm sorry, father," she said, "but there's a man downstairs who insisted I wake you. He said you'd want to see him."

"A man? Who?"

"He said—he said to tell you that Lucky was here."

Now Pickard was awake.

"Lucky?"

"That's right," she said. "Shall I . . . send him away, Father?"

"No," he said, swinging his legs slowly to the floor. God, but when he woke each morning he was stiff! "No," he said, getting painfully to his feet. Elizabeth took hold of his elbow and helped him up. "Where's my robe?"

"Here," she said, picking it up off the foot of the bed.

"All right," he said, taking it from her, "have him wait in my office."

"Wait?"

'Yes, yes, have him wait. And make some coffee, Elizabeth."

"Father, do you know this man? He said you sent for him. Did you . . . did you send for him?"

"Yes, Elizabeth, yes, I sent for him," Pickard said impatiently, "I did. Now, go down and do what I tell you."

"Yes, all right, Father," she said.

She left her father's room as he was putting on his robe. In the hall she saw Elise coming from her room.

"Is something wrong?" Elise asked. "I thought I heard someone at the door."

"Go back to bed, Elise," Elizabeth said. "It's just someone to see your grandfather."

"At this hour?"

"Go back to sleep."

"I can't, I'm awake now. Who is he? What does he want?"

"I don't know. Look, I have to show him to grandfather's office. Why don't you go down and make some coffee?"

"All right."

The two women went downstairs together, and Elise waited by the door while her mother opened it.

When the door opened again, Lucky looked past Elizabeth at the younger woman by the stairs.

"Who is that?"

Elizabeth turned and looked at Elise, then turned back.

"That's my daughter, Mr. Lucky."

"Not Mister Lucky, ma'am," Lucky said. "Just Lucky."

"Whatever you wish," she said. "Will you follow me, please? My father will see you."

"I thought he would."

"This way, please."

Lucky followed Elizabeth into the house and then stopped to exchange glances with Elise, who was staring at him boldly.

"Elise," Elizabeth said, "the coffee?"

"Yes, Mother."

Elise went into the kitchen, and Lucky followed Elizabeth to Evan Pickard's office.

"Have a seat, Mister—uh—Lucky, and my father will be down in a minute."

"Thank you."

"I'll have coffee for you shortly."

"I appreciate it, ma'am."

She nodded and started for the door.

"Ma'am?"

"Yes?"

"I'm sorry if I sounded rude before."

"That's all right . . . Lucky, there's no need to apologize."

As she left Lucky sat back and thought about the younger woman he had seen by the stairs. The older woman would surely be more experienced, but there was something about the young ones . . .

Evan Pickard walked into his office and strode to his desk.

"You made good time," he said to Lucky.

"You said there'd be extra money in it if I did," Lucky said, reminding him.

"And I meant it," Pickard said, sitting down. "Did you bring that partner of yours with you?"

"Morgan? Yeah, he's along. Why?"

"Because this one might take the two of you."

Lucky's eyebrows went up and he said, "What'd you do, get the ghost of Bill Hickok mad at you?"

"Worse than that."

Lucky snorted derisively and said, "The only thing worse than that would be—" and then he stopped short.

"That's right, Lucky," the Judge said, "the Gunsmith."

Lucky and Pickard stared at one another for a few moments, and then Lucky said, "You were right."

"About what?"

"About this one costing extra," Lucky said, "a lot extra."

Clint woke first and eased out from beneath Sandra's arms and legs without waking her. Standing next to the bed he looked down at her and marveled at how much younger she looked with her face in complete repose.

He walked to the window and then remembered that it only overlooked the alley. Leaning over he could see part of the street, but not enough to tell him anything.

"What are you looking for?" she asked from the bed.

"Nothing in particular," he said, turning to face her.

She pulled the sheet away from her to reveal her nakedness to him.

"Maybe I can give you something to look for," she said, invitingly.

"Yeah," he said, approaching the bed, "maybe you can, at that . . ."

TWENTY-EIGHT

Instead of having breakfast with Clint, Sandra said she was going to go to her room and get some more sleep.

"I didn't get all that much rest last night, you know."

"Believe me," he said, "I know."

They went down to the lobby together, where they separated. Sandra left to go to her room and Clint went to the desk to talk to Wisler.

"Well, well . . ." Wisler said, grinning at Clint.

"What's that grin for?"

"In town a few days and already you've gotten through to the Ice Princess."

"Ice Princess?"

"If you only knew how many men have tried to get to know her out from behind her blackjack table. How did you mange to do it?"

"Charm, I guess," Clint said. "Tell me something, George."

"What?"

"Does Pickard own the telegraph office?"

"No, why?"

"I'd like to send a message to a friend of mine in Texas."

"What for?"

"He's got a lot of connections. I'd like to find out what kind of judge Pickard was."

"I can tell you that," Wisler said. "He was a crooked judge, plain and simple. He had a price, and it was high, but he could be bought."

"Is that how he built his fortune?"

"That and other crooked ways. I told you, he resigned just ahead of a warrant."

"What about the key operator?"

"I'd say he was firmly in Pickard's pocket. If you had him send a message, it'd be on Pickard's desk less than five minutes later."

"Well, I guess that's out, then."

"Unless you can find somebody else who can work a telegraph key."

The crafty glint in Wisler's eye told Clint that the man did know another key operator.

"Are you going to tell me, or do I have to guess? Who's a key operator?"

"I am," Wisler said. "All we have to do is get the regular operator out of the way for a couple of minutes."

"You got a paper and pencil?"

Wisler produced both from beneath the desk.

While Clint was writing out his message to his friend Rick Hartman in Labyrinth, Texas, Wisler asked, "What about the answer?"

"Rick will have to answer me in some sort of code

that he knows I can figure out. It won't be unusual for me to receive a telegraph message."

"Maybe you should send a second one with the regular operator, so it really doesn't look funny when you receive one."

Clint looked at Wisler and said, "That's a good idea, George."

"When do you want to do this?"

"Whenever you're available," Clint said. "You'll need someone to watch the desk for you, won't you?"

"I'll get Willy."

"Who's Willy?"

"The town drunk, but that's okay. All I need is a warm body behind here to shove the register at people—if anyone comes in."

"What time's the telegraph office open?" Clint asked.

"At nine."

"That's what I thought. I guess I'll have some breakfast and meet you back here. I'd invite you to eat with me, but I don't think we should be seen together."

"I agree. Everybody knows how I feel about Pickard."

"I'll be back here at ten minutes to nine," Clint said, handing Wisler the message. "I'll get the key operator away from the office and you send this."

Wisler took the piece of paper and nodded.

Clint started to leave, then turned back and asked, "Where is the office, George?"

"Right on Main Street," Wisler said. "You thinking about breaking in and using the key?"

"The thought had occurred to me, but what would the chances be that there'd be somebody on the other side before nine?"

"Also, it wouldn't be easy to break in and go un-noticed, not right out on Main Street."

"All right, then," Clint said, "I'll meet you back here in under an hour."

"I'll be waiting."

After Clint left, Wisler read the message he was to send:

R.H.
NEED INFORMATION ON JUDGE EVAN PIC-
KARD, HARRISON LEGGETT, AND PHIL SAD-
LER. SEND REPLY SO ONLY I CAN READ IT.
IGNORE SECOND MESSAGE.

C.A.

He tucked the piece of paper into his pocket and thought about the last time he'd operated a telegraph key. He fervently hoped he still remembered how.

Ah, as soon as he sat down at the key it would come back to him.

He hoped.

While Clint Adams was sitting down to breakfast, Lucas Lucky was putting an empty coffee cup on Judge Pickard's desk.

"You've got a real nice house here, Judge," he commented.

"There's only one reason I've tolerated you coming here, Lucky, and that's because I want this job done right, and I want it done soon."

"You've got a real pretty daughter, Judge," Lucky said, "and an even prettier granddaughter. Thank them for the coffee for me, will you?"

"Now listen here—"

"Oh," Lucky said, "I'm gonna need something in advance, Judge. After all, we're gonna have to get us a couple of rooms."

"You're not staying at the hotel, are you?"

"Rooming house, like always."

Pickard opened the top drawer of his desk and took out some money. He counted some out and handed it to Lucky. As the younger man reached for it, Pickard pulled it back.

"Stay away from my daughter and my granddaughter, Lucky—you and your partner. You got that?"

"I understand, Judge," Lucky said. "We're good enough to kill for you, but not good enough to associate with you and yours."

"Now you've got it straight," Pickard said, handing him the money. "Remember, I want it done soon."

"You don't want me to shoot him in the back, do you?"

"I want you to do it any way you can get it done," the Judge said. "I want Clint Adams dead."

"Why do you want this one so bad, Judge? Why does Adams' presence in town put you in such a sweat?"

"That's none of your business, Lucky," Pickard said, shortly. "Just do what I'm paying you to do."

"Oh, it'll get done, Judge," Lucky said, moving toward the door. "It will get done."

Lucky left the office and walked down the hall to the front door. Coming down the steps was Elise Pickard, dressed in riding clothes. Lucky thought she looked wonderful in jeans and boots.

"Well," he said, "I was afraid I was going to have to see myself to the door."

Elise came up to him and boldly took hold of his arm.

"We couldn't have that," she said, "could we?"

TWENTY-NINE

After breakfast Clint found a little boy about eleven and paid him a quarter to do an errand for him. He told the boy to meet him at the hotel afterward and he'd pay him another two bits. After that he went to the hotel to meet Wisler.

"Ready?" he asked.

"Ready," Wisler said. "Willy?"

A man came out of the back room wearing clothes that he looked uncomfortable in. His hair was slicked down and parted down the center.

"One of my old suits," Wisler said to Clint. "Remember, Willy, no whiskey until I come back, and then you can have a whole bottle."

"I'll remember, Mr. Wisler," the drunk said, rubbing his hand over his dry lips.

Wisler came back from behind the desk and said, "Let's go."

Clint entered the telegraph office just as the operator was setting up.

"Be with you in a minute, friend," the man said.

He was a portly, balding man in his fifties.

"That's all right," Clint said, "take your time. I'm in no hurry."

After a few minutes of preparation the operator looked up at Clint and said, "All right. Do you have a message you'd like to send?"

"Uh, yes, I do."

Clint had the second message in his pocket, while Wisler had the first. He wondered where the little boy was. If he was forced to send this message first, then Rick would be ignoring the wrong message.

"Now where did I put the damn thing?" Clint said, patting his pockets.

At this point the little boy finally entered the office.

"What do you want?" the key operator asked him. It was obvious the man didn't like children.

The little boy looked at the operator and said, "The Judge wants you."

"What?"

"The Judge wants you," the little boy said, and then with a glance at Clint he turned and ran out.

"What the hell—" the operator said, coming around from behind the desk and rushing to the door.

"That's the damndest thing," Clint said, still patting his pockets.

"Look, have you found that message yet?" the man asked, nervously.

"I have it here somewhere—" Clint said. "Look, who is this Judge, anyway. Somebody important?"

"Um, yes, he is . . ."

"Well, why don't you go see what he wants," Clint

said, "and by the time you get back I'll have found the message."

"You wouldn't mind waiting?"

"Not at all."

The operator rushed behind the desk for his jacket, then to the door again.

"Uh, look here, would you watch the key for me? Don't let anyone fool with it?"

"Of course," Clint said. "I won't let anyone fool with it."

"Thanks," the man said, and rushed off.

Seconds later George Wisler came rushing in.

"All right," he said, moving around behind the desk.

"Send the message," Clint said.

"Wait a second," Wisler said, "I have to sit here a second . . ."

"You said you knew how to operate a key."

"I used to," Wisler said. "It's been a while." He was staring down at the key with great concentration.

"That's great!"

"It'll come back to me," Wisler said, reassuring him. "Watch the door, will you?"

Clint went to the door, fuming.

Click, click, clickety-click.

"Is that it?" Clint asked.

"I think I've got it," Wisler said.

Clickety, clickety, clickety-click.

"Now?"

"Almost."

Click, clickety-click, click-click.

"Well?"

"I've got it."

There were more clicks after that, and Clint was starting to think that maybe Wisler knew what he was doing.

Hopefully.

"That's it," Wisler said, standing up. "I've sent it."

"Did you sent it right?"

Wisler came around the counter and said, "I think so. I either sent your message, or I sent something about Indians."

"Indians?"

"I'm joking," Wisler said. "I sent it."

"I hope you did," Clint said. "You'd better get out of here now."

"I'm going," Wisler said. "We'll know soon enough if I sent the right message."

"I thought you said you did!" Clint hissed at him as he left.

Clint moved away from the door and took a seat. When the operator returned he'd hand him the second message.

Suddenly he jumped up and rushed to the counter. He didn't know much about operating a telegraph key, but he did know that the operator usually left it locked when he was finished using it. Wisler had left it unlocked.

Clint went around the desk, studied it for a few moments, then locked it. He had only just moved back around the counter when the operator came back in.

"Fool boy!" the man said, bitterly. "Practical

jokes.'' He took off his jacket and slammed it down.

"This Judge, he didn't want to see you?"

The man whirled on him, as if he didn't remember leaving him there.

"He didn't know anything about it!" he shouted, then realizing what he'd done, he backed off and said, "Oh, I'm sorry. No reason to shout at you. Did you find that message?"

"Yes, I did," Clint said, taking it out of his shirt pocket. "I have it right here."

THIRTY

When Clint walked into the Pinnacle House Hotel George Wisler was back behind the desk.

'Don't worry,'' Wisler said, reading the look on Clint's face. "It just took me a few moments to get back to it.''

"I hope so.''

"Besides, you've got other things to worry about.''

"Like what?''

"On the way back here I saw someone in town.''

"Who?''

"Somebody who only comes when the Judge calls for him.''

"Are you going to make me guess, George?'' Clint asked. "Who?''

"Lucas Lucky.''

There was a moment of silence while Clint remembered the things he'd heard about Lucas Lucky.

"I see the name rings a bell.''

"It does.''

"One of the new breed, I understand.''

"One of the ones who should have learned from others' mistakes, by now."

"I hear he's good."

"That's what I hear."

"I also hear he travels with a partner, a guy who is supposed to show some promise."

"Name?"

"Mitch Morgan."

"That name doesn't do anything for me."

"It may take a few years for that," Wisler said, "if he lasts that long."

"He won't, if they come after me."

"Are you that confident in your own ability with a gun?" Wisler asked.

Clint didn't answer.

"Yeah," Wisler said, reading his face again, "I guess you are."

"George, I'm going upstairs to get some sleep."

"Sandra didn't let you sleep much, huh?"

"Wake me if I get a telegraph message."

"Sure."

Clint went up to his room, thinking about all the Lucas Luckys and Mitch Morgans he'd already met — and killed — in his life.

Lucas Lucky woke with Elise Pickard lying on his gun arm. Annoyed, he pulled it out from under her head, waking her.

"Hey?" she said. "What time is it?"

"Noon," he said.

She rubbed her eyes and said, "I never would have thought I'd fall asleep."

"You got up early this morning," he said, reminding her.

"Oh," she said, "so I did."

She rolled over on top of him and took him inside of her. While she was riding his rigid penis he reached out to make sure he could touch his gun.

"Take it out," she said.

"Finished already?"

"No," she said, breathlessly, "take the gun out."

"Why?"

"It excites me."

"You need that to get excited?" he asked. "I didn't notice that before."

"Please . . ." she moaned, crushing herself down on him.

He shrugged and removed the gun from the holster.

"Have you ever killed anyone?" she asked.

"Lots of people."

"Ooh, really?" she asked, biting her bottom lip.

"Sure," he said.

"Where do you shoot them?"

He pressed the barrel of the gun against her left nipple and said, "Right in the heart."

"Ooh!"

He turned the gun so that her nipple was right inside the barrel. As he did so she groaned loudly and arched her back, spasms of pleasure wracking her body.

He turned her over then and drove himself into her, seeking his own release. He kept the gun in his hand, pressing the cold metal against her breast so hard that by the time he was spent the impression of the gun was on her skin.

"Oooh," she said, rubbing her hand over it, "that was delicious."

"You're a little strange, aren't you?" he said, sitting up and putting his feet on the floor.

"I never noticed before," she said, still rubbing the skin of her breast, "but I suppose you're right."

He stood up and reached for his pants.

"Are you here to kill someone?"

"Maybe," he said, buttoning his pants.

"Who?"

He didn't answer. Once he had his pants on, he reached for his makings and built himself a cigarette.

"Are you here to kill my grandfather?"

"Would you pay me to?"

"What?"

"I like to be paid when I kill someone."

"Is that necessary?"

"Not always," he said, "but it helps."

"How much do you get paid?"

"That depends on who I'm killing."

"You don't give away much, do you?"

"No," he said, "not for free."

"I wouldn't call this," she said, tossing the sheet aside so he could see her body, "for free."

"No," he said. "I wouldn't, either. Who do you want me to kill?"

"Would you really kill someone for me?"

"Yes."

"Just for my body?"

"Yes."

"Why?"

He shrugged.

"It's as good a reason as any."

He picked up his shirt and put it on.

"You haven't slept," she said. "You rode all night and you haven't slept. Come to bed."

"I dozed."

"An hour? Maybe two?"

"That's all I need," he said.

He took his gun off the bedpost and strapped it on.

"Are you fast?"

"Fast enough," he said, making sure it settled properly on his hips.

"Faster than . . . the Gunsmith?"

"I don't know," he said. "He's pretty fast."

She stared at him and asked, "Are you here to kill him?"

He didn't answer.

"Boy, you don't give anything away with your face or your eyes."

"I have to go out," he said, putting on his leather vest. "Stay or go home."

"You don't care which?" she asked as he went to the door.

"No," he said, and left.

She lay back on the bed, staring at the ceiling and absently rubbing at the mark his gun had left on her breast. He had been fine in bed, but it was still Clint that she wanted. If she warned Clint that Lucky was here to kill him, would he take her to bed?

It was worth a try.

THIRTY-ONE

Clint was awakened by a knocking at his door.

"Yeah!" he called, struggling off the bed. Jesus, but all of a sudden he was tired.

"It's George," Wisler called. "You got your message."

"Yeah," Clint said, again. Wearing only his pants he walked to the door and opened it.

"Here," Wisler said, holding it out to him. "I don't know what it says."

Clint took the slip of paper and read it:

C.A.
ONE WALKS A CROOKED ROAD.
TWO IS A MYSTERY.
THREE'S FAVORITE COLOR IS PINK,
AND FOUR IS MISSING.

R.H.

"What does it mean?" Wisler asked. "I mean, 'One walks a crooked road' is sort of self-explanatory."

"Judge Pickard's a crook."

"And 'Two is unknown' is plain."

"He doesn't know Leggett."

"What the hell does 'Three's favorite color is pink,' mean?" Wisler asked.

Clint rubbed his jaw.

"If I read this right—and I think I do—my deceased friend Phil Sadler was a Pinkerton."

"A detective?" Wisler said. "Well, that makes sense, now. He was a detective on his way here to get the goods on Judge Pickard."

"But who hired him?" Clint said. "Leggett?"

"Who else?" Wisler said. "Why else would he send you here to find Leggett?"

"I don't know," Clint said. "There's still a lot that's unknown here."

"Yeah, but a lot is clearing up, too," Wisler said. "Whatever crookedness the Judge is up to lately Leggett found out about it and sent for a Pinkerton man. Unfortunately, Pickard found out about it and had the Pinkerton man killed, and then had Leggett killed—or the other way around. Either way, they're both dead."

Clint had to admit that Wisler's summation made a lot of sense. Still, he wasn't convinced that Leggett was the only choice to have sent for the Pinkerton man.

There was also George Wisler himself.

"I know what you're thinking," Wisler said.

"What?"

"That I sent for the Pinkerton."

"George, you amaze me sometimes."

"That wasn't hard to figure, Clint," Wisler said.

"Believe me, if I had sent for a Pinkerton I wouldn't have any reason to lie about it."

"I suppose not."

"And there's no one else in this town with any reason to."

Clint hesitated, then repeated, "I suppose not."

"Well, well . . ." Wisler said, looking down the hall.

Clint leaned out to look down the hall and saw Elizabeth Pickard coming down the hall.

"If Sandra comes by," Wisler said under his breath, "I'll tell her to wait her turn."

Clint frowned as Wisler went down the hall past Elizabeth, muttering a greeting.

"Clint," she said, when she reached his door.

"Elizabeth," he said. "Excuse me, but I'm not dressed for company."

"That's all right," she said, looking him up and down, "you look fine. May I come in?"

He tried to read the look in her eyes.

"I'd like to talk to you."

"Sure," he said, backing up to allow her to enter. "Come on in."

THIRTY-TWO

Lucky knocked on Mitch Morgan's door.

"Go 'way," Morgan's muffled voice called from inside.

"Come on, Morgan," Lucky said. "We've got work to do."

"Later." Again, Morgan's voice sounded oddly muffled.

"Come on, Mitch!" Lucky said, banging on the door.

He heard feet hit the floor and pound angrily to the door, and then the door was flung open. Morgan was naked, and his manhood was aroused. The lower portion of his face was wet, and behind him on the bed a young girl lay, her legs wide open. She looked to be about sixteen, slender, with hardly any breasts, long blonde hair, and hair the color of wheat between her slender thighs.

"Now where the hell did you get her?" Lucky asked.

"She came by to clean the room," Morgan said. "Where did you get yours?"

"Mitch!" the girl wailed. Obviously, they had not finished what they started. "Please, Mitch!"

"Lucky . . ."

"All right," Lucky said. "Finish up and meet me outside."

"Where?"

"The nearest saloon."

"It's only noon."

"I'm still thirsty."

"All right," Morgan said. "Ten minutes."

"Mitch!"

"Maybe twenty . . ."

"I don't have anything to offer you," Clint said.

"That's all right."

She was wearing a simple dress that buttoned all the way to her neck.

"What's wrong, Elizabeth?"

"I don't know," she said, "and I don't know why I'm coming to you."

"You need someone to talk to."

"Yes," she said, "I do."

"Sit down."

She sat on the bed and he sat next to her. Their thighs were touching, and he could feel the heat of her through her clothes.

"A man came to the house this morning, early."

"And?"

"He made me wake my father, said that Father had sent for him."

"And had he?"

"Yes."

"What's bothering you about it?"

"The man . . . he looked like a killer."

"What's a killer look like, Elizabeth?"

"You know what I mean," Elizabeth said. "It was obvious that he'd ridden all night to get here, and my father was agitated when I told him he was downstairs. They stayed in his office for quite a while, and when the man left, he was putting money in his pocket."

"Is that all?"

"No," she said, with a heavy sigh. "No, it's not. He also left with Elise. They didn't see me, but I saw them."

"Is that what's really bothering you, then?"

"I don't know," she said, her shoulders slumping. "I guess not knowing what's going on is bothering me. First you show up, asking about Harrison Leggett and getting Father all upset, and now this."

"You do know Leggett?"

"Yes, he was my father's accountant."

"What happened to him?"

"Father said he caught him stealing from him and fired him."

"Elizabeth, don't read anything into what I'm about to ask you, but does that sound like your father to you?"

"No," she said, without hesitation. She looked at Clint then and said, "He killed him, didn't he, Clint— or had him killed?"

"I think so."

"By this man who came to the house today?"

"Possibly," Clint said.

"Clint, what are you doing here?"

He decided to tell her. He explained how he found Phil Sadler and how Sadler's dying words had sent him here to find Harrison Leggett.

"You think my father had this man Sadler killed?"

"Yes."

"But . . . why?"

"I've just found out that Sadler was a Pinkerton man."

"I don't understand any of this," Elizabeth said. "My father was a judge! Why should he be killing people now?"

"My information is that your father was never a very honest judge, Elizabeth," Clint said. "Did he ever tell you why he left the bench?"

"He said he was getting tired of it and that he wanted to make a fortune in private life without anyone questioning his honesty."

"Well, they are questioning it," Clint said. "I think Leggett sent for Sadler, and your father had them both killed."

"What are you going to do?"

"I don't know," he said. "I can't prove anything. I can't even prove that Harrison Leggett is dead."

There was a long moment's hesitation and then she said, "I can."

"What?"

"I saw them . . ."

"You saw them kill him?"

"No. I saw that young boy, Hicks, and some burly men loading a body onto a buckboard behind the saloon."

"Which saloon?"

"My father's," she said, "the Cold Cash."

"You didn't see this man, the one who was at your house this morning?"

"No."

"How did you know the body was Leggett's?"

"I recognized him. There was a full moon that night and I saw his face."

"What were you doing out that night?"

"I was . . . going to meet . . . someone."

"Who?" he asked, before he realized that it was none of his business.

"The sheriff," she said. "Sheriff Haskell."

Haskell was a little younger than Elizabeth, but that didn't really matter.

"All right," he said. "That part's none of my business."

"I'm involved with him, Clint," she said. "Nobody knows about it, but that was another reason why I couldn't . . . couldn't see you . . ."

"It's all right, Elizabeth," he said. "Hicks works for your father, right?"

"Yes."

"Would you testify that you saw Hicks and some other men loading Leggett's body onto a buckboard?"

"He's my father, Clint . . ."

"I know," he said. "It's a tough decision."

"I-I can't decide—"

"Why don't you talk it over with Haskell?"

She looked at him then with tear-filled eyes and said, "That's a good idea."

"Go and do it now."

She leaned over and kissed him on the cheek.

"Thank you Clint," she said. "If it wasn't for . . ."

"Go on," he said. "I'll respect your decision, Elizabeth."

"You'll still go after my father, even if I don't testify?"

"It'll be harder, but yes."

"I—I'll try to make the right decision."

They were both on their feet when there was a knock on the door. Clint opened the door and saw Elise Pickard. Elise saw him, and then saw her mother standing slightly behind him.

"Oh," she said, pouting, "I see . . ."

"Don't be an ass, Elise," her mother said. "Thank you, Clint, for listening."

"Anytime, Elizabeth."

As her mother walked down the hall, Elise said to Clint, "For listening? Is that all you did?"

"Whether you believe it or not, that's all."

They were both silent for a few moments, and then Clint said, "Do you want to come in?"

"Yes," she said, "thank you."

He allowed her to enter and closed the door.

"What brings you here?"

"I have something to tell you."

"All right."

"There's a man in town, a killer, and he means to kill you."

"Lucky."

"You know about him?" she asked, surprised.

"Yes. Did he tell you that?"

"No, but when I asked him if he was here to kill someone, he said 'maybe'. Clint, I think my grandfather hired him to kill you.''

"Probably.''

"Will you kill him?''

"I hope it won't come to that.''

"He's got another man with him.''

"Thanks very much for the warning, Elise. I appreciate it.''

"I just wanted to show you . . . that I care,'' she said, moving closer to him.

He took her by the shoulders and kissed her. He meant it as a friendly gesture, but her tongue avidly darted into his mouth and the kiss went on for some time.

"You want me,'' she said, breathlessly.

"What man wouldn't?'' he asked.

"Now?''

"No,'' he said, shaking his head, "not now.''

He pulled on his shirt and strapped on his gun, reminding her of Lucky.

"Do you know where he is, Elise?''

"The Cold Cash.''

He nodded and headed for the door.

"Clint,'' she said as he went to the door.

"Yes?''

"Don't you dare get killed.''

"I'll try not to.''

"You're a busy man,'' George Wisler said as Clint came down. "It's a wonder you can walk.''

"Get your mind off your crotch, George. Are you any kind of a hand with a gun?''

"None at all,'' he said. "If I didn't have a shotgun

I wouldn't hit anything. You need some backup?"

"It would help."

"Let me get my shotgun."

"You need someone to watch the desk?"

"To hell with the desk," Wisler said. He went into the back room and came out with the shotgun. "I wouldn't miss this for the world."

"Just watch my back, George."

"I'll watch it," Wisler said, "and I'll blow the head off anyone who tries to ventilate it."

"That's what I mean," Clint said.

THIRTY-THREE

It hadn't mattered to Lucas Lucky that the saloon wasn't open for business yet.

"The doors are open," he said to the bartender.

"Yeah, but we ain't really open."

"Just give me a whiskey, son," Lucky said.

"Uh—y-yes sir!"

Lucky was nursing the whiskey when Clint Adams walked in. He walked to the other end of the bar and called the bartender over.

"Uh, we ain't really open," the bartender said, trying again.

"You gave him a drink," Clint said, "you can give me one."

The bartender grinned nervously and said, "What'll you have?"

"What he's having," Clint said. "In fact, he's buying." •

The bartender looked at Lucky, who hadn't looked over at Clint at all yet.

Normally, Clint would have left it for a man like

Lucky to come looking for him, but he figured to throw him off balance this way and maybe avoid the inevitable—if that was possible.

When Clint had his drink, the bartender walked down the bar, past Lucky and ducked into the back room.

"Adams?" Lucky finally said.

"That's right."

"Making my job easy, aren't you?"

"If you think killing a man is easy," Clint said, "you're a fool."

"Killing a man is easy," Lucky said, still leaning on the bar, "sometimes it's finding him that's hard."

"I'm here," Clint said. "You don't have to try and find me."

"Like I said," Lucky said straightening up, "making my job easy."

Lucky turned toward Clint and dripped his hand off the bar. The move was meant to look like he was clearing the bar, getting ready to draw, but in reality his hand just kept going to his gun.

Usually, when Clint had a man clearly beat, he was able to follow the man's hand to his gun, as if the man was moving in slow motion. That wasn't the case with Lucas Lucky. The man's move was excellent, and he had even cleared leather by the time Clint shot him.

Lucky staggered against the bar, his gun dropping from his hand, and then slid to the floor.

Clint holstered his gun as George Wisler entered the saloon.

"I watched from the window," Wisler said. "You *are* as good as they say."

"He was good," Clint said.

"You were better."

"That's the whole idea."

At that point a young man entered the saloon on the run, shouting, "Lucky!"

He stopped short when he saw Lucky on the floor. He rushed to the body, bent over it, and then looked up at Clint.

"You killed him!"

"He didn't give me a choice, son."

The boy—who Clint assumed by now was Mitch Morgan—stood up.

"I ain't giving you a choice either, Adams."

"I'm giving you one, son," Clint said, holding his left hand out to Wisler to keep him from doing anything foolish.

"Stay alive and bury your friend," Clint said.

"He was more than my friend," Morgan said. "I—I was supposed to be here with him, instead I was in bed with—with—I shoulda been here, don't you understand?"

"I understand, son," Clint said. "I understand your grief, but your dying isn't going to bring him back, is it?"

"I'm gonna kill you!"

"You can't, son," Clint said. "Were you as fast as he was? Look at him."

"He was the best!" Morgan said through gritted teeth.

"And look where he ended up."

Reluctantly, Morgan's eyes shifted from Clint to the fallen Lucky. At that point the sheriff came charging in with his gun out, spooking Morgan. The boy went for his gun and Clint shouted, "No!" wanting to keep Wisler and Haskell from firing.

He leaped forward and caught the boy's hand as he grabbed his gun.

"Leave it there, Mitch," Clint said. "It's over."

Morgan stared at Clint and then moved his hand away from his gun. Clint removed the gun and held it out to the sheriff, who stepped forward and took it.

"The one on the floor drew on me," Clint said. "I think you'll find out that these men killed Harrison Leggett, on the order of Judge Pickard."

Haskell didn't show surprise. Obviously, he had talked with Elizabeth.

"What are you talking about?" Morgan said.

"The man you and your friend killed last month."

"We wasn't even here last month," Morgan said, bending over Lucky again.

"Where were you?" Clint asked, frowning.

"Mexico."

"Can you prove it?" Haskell asked.

"Yeah, I can prove it."

"I'll take him over to the office and we'll get this sorted out."

"I'll join you there later," Clint said.

"Where are you going?" Haskell said.

"To see the Judge."

Clint started for the door, then turned and said to

the sheriff, "Get him over to the undertaker's. I want to make sure he gets a decent burial."

Morgan turned his tear-stained face up to Clint and said, "Thanks, Mister."

It seemed an odd thing to say to the man who had just killed your best friend.

THIRTY-FOUR

Walking to Pickard's office, Clint marvelled at how dense he had been. Suddenly, Sadler's cryptic message to Leggett made all the sense in the world.

Clint stormed into Pickard's outer office and slammed his door open without knocking.

"What the hell—" Pickard said. He was seated and tried to rise quickly, but his aching legs failed him and he remained seated. In the room with him, standing next to the desk, was another person Clint wanted very much to see.

"I'm glad you're here," Clint said. "I sure let you play me for a fool."

"Don't feel bad," Sandra Stone said. "It's happened before. If it's any consolation, I really enjoyed our time together."

"Yeah, so did I," Clint said, "otherwise this wouldn't bother me."

"What is this about?" Pickard asked.

"Oh, never mind, Evan," Sandra said. "He's figured it out." She looked at Clint and said, "What happened to Lucky?"

"He's dead," Clint said. "He wasn't as good as he thought he was."

"And Morgan?"

"He's with the sheriff, probably talking about killing Phil Sadler."

"And Harrison Leggett?" she asked.

"You know better than that, Sandra," Clint said. "You killed Leggett."

"You see?" she said, turning toward Pickard. "He's figured it out, like I told you."

When she turned back to Clint she was holding her derringer, but she was surprised to see that Clint was also holding his gun.

"I've seen you move with that thing, Sandra," Clint said, "so you're not surprising me."

She stared at him for a few moments, then shrugged and put the derringer down on the desk.

"How did you figure it out?"

"I should have known a long time ago, as soon as we met. Before Sadler died, he asked me to tell Leggett to 'Watch out for . . . dealer's choice.' Obviously, he didn't get all the words out, but he did say 'dealer,' and that was you. Somehow, Sadler had found out that you were working for Pickard as more than just a dealer."

"His ace in the hole, he called me," she said, looking at the old man without fondness.

"Why did you shoot at the men who were working me over?" he asked curiously.

"I didn't know they were Pickard's," she said. "The old man's getting a little senile, and he didn't tell me what he'd planned."

"Who's senile?" Pickard demanded. "Listen here, young lady—"

"Shut up, you old fool!" she said. "Can't you see it's all over?" She looked at Clint and said, "He built this damn town up just so he could steal from the townspeople. He's been taking their money from the bank for years."

"How did you start with him, Sandra?"

She laughed and said, "I started out as his own private whore. Believe me, the happiest day of my life was when he couldn't get hard anymore."

"And you worked your way up to being his partner."

"I don't have any partners, Adams," he said. "I run my own business."

"You couldn't run a medicine show—" she started to say, but what happened next was so unexpected that it caught both her and Clint flat-footed.

The old man picked up her derringer and shot her in the left breast.

Her eyes widened and she looked down at the bloody hole in shock.

"You old fool . . ." she said, and fell to the floor.

"Who's an old fool?" Pickard said.

"Put it down Pickard!"

"Fuck you, Adams," the man said. Then he cackled, put the derringer in his mouth and pulled the other trigger.

Watch for

RIDE FOR VENGEANCE

eighty-seventh novel in the exciting
GUNSMITH series

coming in March!

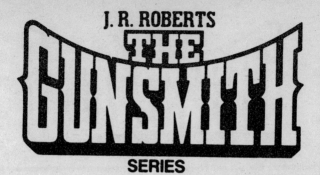

J. R. ROBERTS
THE GUNSMITH
SERIES

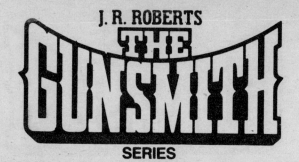

THE GUNSMITH

SERIES